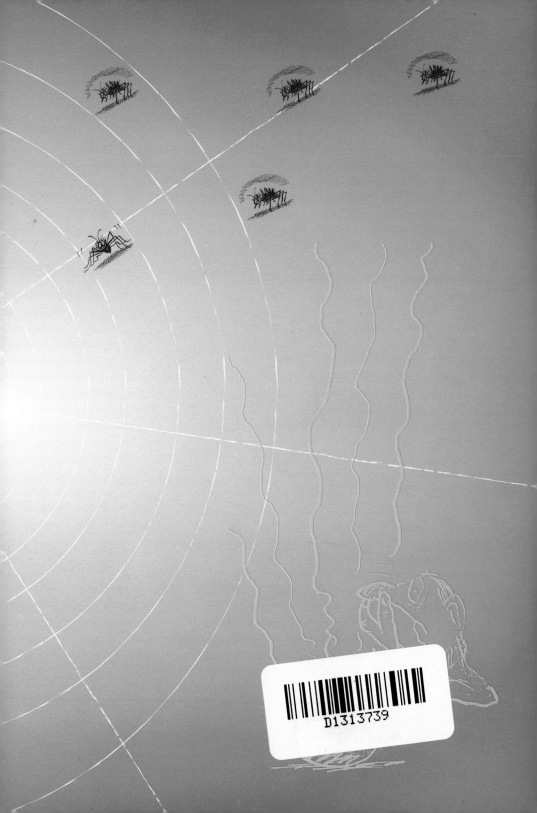

HORRID HENRY'S EVIL ENEMIES

FRANCESCA SIMON

HORRID HENRY'S EVIL ENEMIES

Illustrated by
Tony Ross

Orion
Children's Books

This book is dedicated to

Hannah & Eve Phillips, Max Pittack,
Raphi Patterson, Sam Rubinstein, Ethan & Jake
Silverstone and Claudia Smith of Akiva School
2006

First published in Great Britain in 2006
by Orion Children's Books
a division of the Orion Publishing Group Ltd
Orion House
5 Upper Saint Martin's Lane
London WC2H 9EA

Text © Francesca Simon and illustrations © Tony Ross
1994, 1996, 1997, 1998, 1999, 2001, 2002, 2004

The Orion Publishing Group's policy is to use papers that are natural,
renewable and recyclable products and made from wood grown in sustainable
forests. The logging and manufacturing processes are expected to conform
to the environmental regulations of the country of origin.

A catalogue record for this book is
available from the British Library.

ISBN-10 1 84255 538 3
ISBN-13 978 1 84255 538 5

Printed in Italy

www.orionbooks.co.uk

CONTENTS

THE USUAL SUSPECTS

HORRID HENRY
AND
MOODY MARGARET

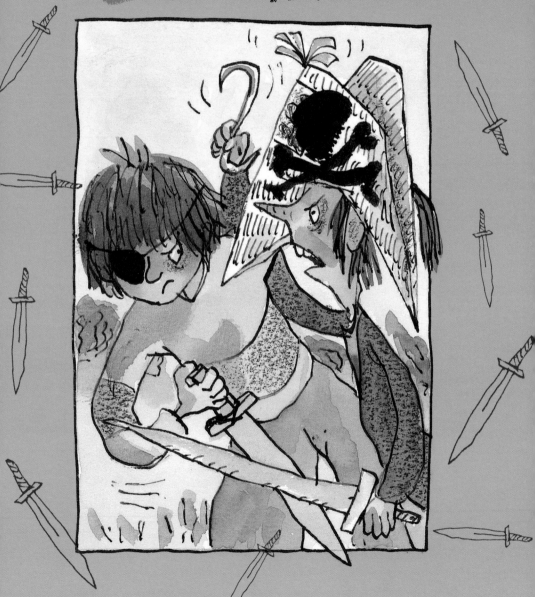

' 'm Captain Hook!'
    'No, I'm Captain Hook!'
'I'm Captain Hook,' said Horrid Henry.
'I'm Captain Hook,' said Moody Margaret.
They glared at each other.
'It's *my* hook,' said Moody Margaret.
    Moody Margaret lived next
door. She did not like Horrid
Henry, and Horrid Henry did
not like her. But when Rude
Ralph was busy, Clever Clare had
flu, and Sour Susan was her
enemy, Margaret would jump
over the wall to play with Henry.

    'Actually, it's my turn to be
Hook now,' said Perfect Peter. 'I've
been the prisoner for such a long
time.'
    'Prisoner, be quiet!' said Henry.
    'Prisoner, walk the plank!' said Margaret.
    'But I've walked it fourteen times already,' said
Peter. 'Please can I be Hook now?'
    'No, by thunder!' said Moody Margaret. 'Now out
of my way, worm!' And she swashbuckled across the
desk, waving her hook and clutching her sword and
dagger.

Margaret had eyepatches and skulls and crossbones and plumed hats and cutlasses and sabres and snickersnees.

Henry had a stick.

This was why Henry played with Margaret.

But Henry had to do terrible things before playing with Margaret's swords. Sometimes he had to sit and wait while she read a book. Sometimes he had to play 'Mums and Dads' with her. Worst of all (please don't tell anyone), sometimes he had to be the baby.

Henry never knew what Margaret would do.

When he put a spider on her arm, Margaret laughed.

When he pulled her hair, Margaret pulled his harder.

When Henry screamed, Margaret would scream louder. Or she would sing. Or pretend not to hear.

Sometimes Margaret was fun. But most of the time she was a moody old grouch.

'I won't play if I can't be Hook,' said Horrid Henry.

Margaret thought for a moment.

'We can both be Captain Hook,' she said.

'But we only have one hook,' said Henry.

'Which I haven't played with yet,' said Peter.

'BE QUIET, prisoner!' shouted Margaret. 'Mr Smee, take him to jail.'

'No,' said Henry.

'You will get your reward, Mr Smee,' said the Captain, waving her hook.

Mr Smee dragged the prisoner to the jail.

'If you're very quiet, prisoner, then you will be freed and you can be a pirate, too,' said Captain Hook.

'Now give me the hook,' said Mr Smee.
The Captain reluctantly handed it over.
'Now I'm Captain Hook and you're Mr
Smee,' shouted Henry. 'I order everyone to walk the
plank!'

'I'm sick of playing pirates,' said Margaret. 'Let's

play something else.'

Henry was furious. That was just like Moody Margaret.

'Well, I'm playing pirates,' said Henry.

'Well I'm not,' said Margaret. 'Give me back my hook.'

'No,' said Henry.

Moody Margaret opened her mouth and screamed. Once Margaret started screaming she could go on and on and on.

Henry gave her the hook.

Margaret smiled.

'I'm hungry,' she said. 'Got anything good to eat?'

Henry had three bags of crisps and seven chocolate biscuits hidden in his room, but he certainly wasn't going to share them with Margaret.

'You can have a radish,' said Henry.

'What else?' said Margaret.

'A carrot,' said Henry.

'What else?' said Margaret.

'Glop,' said Henry.

'What's Glop?'

'Something special that only I can make,' said Henry.

'What's in it?' asked Margaret.

'That's a secret,' said Henry.

'I bet it's yucky,' said Margaret.

'Of course it's yucky.' said Henry.

'I can make the yuckiest Glop of all,' said Margaret.

'That's because you don't know anything. No one can make yuckier Glop than I can.'

'I dare you to eat Glop,' said Margaret.

'I double dare you back,' said Henry. 'Dares go first.'

Margaret stood up very straight.

'All right,' said Margaret. 'Glop starts with snails and worms.'

And she started poking under the bushes.

'Got one!' she shouted, holding up a fat snail.

'Now for some worms,' said Margaret.

She got down on her hands and knees and started digging a hole.

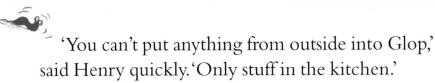

'You can't put anything from outside into Glop,' said Henry quickly. 'Only stuff in the kitchen.'

Margaret looked at Henry.

'I thought we were making Glop,' she said.

'We are,' said Henry. 'My way, because it's *my* house.'

Horrid Henry and Moody Margaret went into the gleaming white kitchen. Henry got out two wooden mixing spoons and a giant red bowl.

'I'll start,' said Henry. He went to the cupboard and opened the doors wide.

'Porridge!' said Henry. And he poured some into the bowl.

Margaret opened the fridge and looked inside. She grabbed a small container.

'Soggy semolina!' shouted Margaret. Into the bowl it went.

'Coleslaw!'

'Spinach!'

'Coffee!'

'Yoghurt!'

'Flour!'

'Vinegar!'

'Baked beans!'

'Mustard!'

'Peanut butter!'

'Mouldy cheese!'

'Pepper!'

'Rotten oranges!'

'And ketchup!' shouted Henry.

He squirted in the ketchup until the bottle was empty.

'Now, mix!' said Margaret.

Horrid Henry and Moody Margaret grabbed hold of their spoons with both hands. Then they plunged the spoons into the Glop and began to stir.

It was hard heavy work.

Faster and faster, harder and harder they stirred.

There was Glop on the ceiling. There was Glop on the floor. There was Glop on the clock, and Glop on the door. Margaret's hair was covered in Glop. So was Henry's face.

Margaret looked into the bowl. She had never seen anything so yucky in her life.

'It's ready,' she said.

Horrid Henry and Moody Margaret carried the Glop to the table.

Then they sat down and stared at the sloppy, slimy, sludgy, sticky, smelly, gooey, gluey, gummy, greasy, gloopy Glop.

'Right,' said Henry. 'Who's going to eat some first?'

There was a very long pause.

Henry looked at Margaret.

Margaret looked at Henry.

'Me,' said Margaret. 'I'm not scared.'

She scooped up a large spoonful and stuffed it in her mouth.

Then she swallowed. Her face went pink and purple and green.

'How does it taste?' said Henry.

'Good,' said Margaret, trying not to choke.

'Have some more then,' said Henry.

'Your turn first,' said Margaret.

Henry sat for a moment and looked at the Glop.

'My mum doesn't like me to eat between meals,' said Henry.

'HENRY!' hissed Moody Margaret.

Henry took a tiny spoonful.

'More!' said Margaret.

Henry took a tiny bit more. The Glop wobbled lumpily on his spoon. It looked like . . . Henry did not want to think about what it looked like.

He closed his eyes and brought the spoon to his mouth.

'Ummm, yummm,' said Henry.

'You didn't eat any,' said Margaret. 'That's not fair.'

She scooped up some Glop and . . .

I dread to think what would have happened next, if they had not been interrupted.

'Can I come out now?' called a small voice from outside. 'It's my turn to be Hook.'

Horrid Henry had forgotten all about Perfect Peter.

'OK,' shouted Henry.

Peter came to the door.

'I'm hungry,' he said.

'Come in, Peter,' said Henry sweetly. 'Your dinner is on the table.'

SPECIAL GLOP RECIPES

Wormy Glop

Worms
Beetroot
Mud
Vinegar
Salt

Rotten Glop

Banana **peel**
Rotten **lemons**
Cold **porridge**
Horseradish
Cola

Toothpaste Glop

Lumpy custard
Brussels sprouts
peelings
Toothpaste
Yoghurt
Mustard

HORRID HENRY'S TOP SECRET UNBREAKABLE CODE

A = Z	J = Q	S = H
B = Y	K = P	T = G
C = X	L = O	U = F
D = W	M = N	V = E
E = V	N = M	W = D
F = U	O = L	X = C
G = T	P = K	Y = B
H = S	Q = J	Z = A
I = R	R = I	

HNVOOBTLZWYILGSVIHPVVKLFG.

WARNING:

DO NOT LOOK on page 166!

HORRID HENRY
AND THE
SECRET CLUB

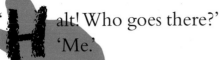

'**H**alt! Who goes there?'

'Me.'

'Who's me?' said Moody Margaret.

'ME!' said Sour Susan.

'What's the password?'

'Uhhhh . . .' Sour Susan paused. What was the password? She thought and thought and thought.

'Potatoes?'

Margaret sighed loudly. Why was she friends with such a stupid person?

'No it isn't.'

'Yes it is,' said Susan.

'Potatoes was last week's password,' said Margaret.

'No it wasn't.'

'Yes it was,' said Moody Margaret. 'It's my club and I decide.'

There was a long pause.

'All right,' said Susan sourly. 'What *is* the password?'

'I don't know if I'm going to tell you,' said Margaret. 'I could be giving away a big secret to the enemy.'

'But I'm not the enemy,' said Susan. 'I'm Susan.'

'Shhhh!' said Margaret. 'We don't want Henry to find out who's in the secret club.'

Susan looked quickly over her shoulder. The enemy was nowhere to be seen. She whistled twice.

'All clear,' said Sour Susan. 'Now let me in.'

Moody Margaret thought for a moment. Letting someone in without the password broke the first club rule.

'Prove to me you're Susan, and not the enemy pretending to be Susan,' said Margaret.

'You know it's me,' wailed Susan.

'Prove it.'

Susan stuck her foot into the tent.

'I'm wearing the black patent leather shoes with the blue flowers I always wear.'

'No good,' said Margaret. 'The enemy could have stolen them.'

'I'm speaking with Susan's voice and I look like Susan,' said Susan.

'No good,' said Margaret. 'The enemy could be a master of disguise.'

Susan stamped her foot. 'And I know that you were the one who pinched Helen and I'm going to tell Miss . . .'

'Come closer to the tent flap,' said Margaret.

Susan bent over.

'Now listen to me,' said Margaret. 'Because I'm only going to tell you once. When a secret club member wants to come in they say NUNGA. Anyone inside answers back, 'Nunga Nu.' That's how I know it's you and you know it's me.'

'**NUNGA,**' said Sour Susan.

'**NUNGA NU,**' said Moody Margaret. 'Enter.'

Susan entered the club. She gave the secret handshake, sat down on her box and sulked.

'You knew it was me all along,' said Susan.

Margaret scowled at her.

'That's not the point. If you don't want to obey the club rules you can leave.'

Susan didn't move.

'Can I have a biscuit?' she said.

Margaret smiled graciously. 'Have two,' she said. 'Then we'll get down to business.'

Meanwhile, hidden under a bush behind some strategically placed branches, another top secret meeting was taking place in the next door garden.

'I think that's everything,' said the Leader. 'I shall now put the plans into action.'

'What am I going to do?' said Perfect Peter.

'Stand guard,' said Horrid Henry.

'I always have to stand guard,' said Peter, as the Leader crept out.

'It's not fair.'

'Have you brought your spy report?' asked Margaret.

'Yes,' said Susan.

'Read it aloud,' said Margaret.

Susan took out a piece of paper and read:

'I watched the enemy's house for two hours yesterday morning –'

'Which morning?' interrupted Margaret.

'Saturday morning,' said Susan. 'A lady with grey

hair and a beret walked past.'

'What colour was the beret?' said Margaret.

'I don't know,' said Susan.

'Call yourself a spy and you don't know what colour the beret was,' said Margaret.

'Can I please continue with my report?' said Susan.

'I'm not stopping you,' said Margaret.

'Then I saw the enemy leave the house with his brother and mother. The enemy kicked his brother twice. His mother shouted at him. Then I saw the postman –'

'**NUNGA!**' screeched a voice from outside.

Margaret and Susan froze.

'**NUNGA!!!**' screeched the voice again. 'I know you're in there!'

'Aaaahh!' squeaked Susan. 'It's Henry!'

'Quick! Hide!' hissed Margaret.

The secret spies crouched behind two boxes.

'You told him our password!' hissed Margaret. 'How dare you!'

'Wasn't me!' hissed Susan. 'I couldn't even remember it, so how could I have told him? You told him!'

'Didn't,' hissed Margaret.

'NUNGA!!!' screeched Henry again. 'You have to let me in! I know the password.'

'What do we do?' hissed Susan. 'You said anyone who knows the password enters.'

'For the last time, NUNGAAAAA!' shouted Horrid Henry.

'Nunga Nu,' said Margaret. 'Enter.'

Henry swaggered into the tent. Margaret glared at him.

'Don't mind if I do,' said Henry, grabbing all the chocolate biscuits and stuffing them into his mouth. Then he sprawled on the rug, scattering crumbs everywhere.

'What are you doing?' said Horrid Henry.

'Nothing,' said Moody Margaret.

'Nothing,' said Sour Susan.

'You are, too,' said Henry.

'Mind your own business,' said Margaret. 'Now, Susan, let's vote on whether to allow boys in. I vote No.'

'I vote No, too,' said Susan.

'Sorry, Henry, you can't join. Now leave.'

'No,' said Henry.

'LEAVE,' said Margaret.

'Make me,' said Henry.

Margaret took a deep breath. Then she opened her mouth and screamed. No one could scream as loud, or as long, or as piercingly, as Moody Margaret. After a few moments, Susan started screaming too.

Henry got to his feet, knocking over the crate they used as a table.

'Watch out,' said Henry. 'Because the Purple Hand will be back!' He turned to go.

Moody Margaret sprang up behind him and pushed him through the flap. Henry landed in a heap outside.

'Can't get me!' shouted Henry. He picked himself up and jumped over the wall. 'The Purple Hand is the best!'

'Oh yeah,' muttered Margaret. 'We'll see about that.'

Henry checked over his shoulder to make sure no one was watching. Then he crept back to his fort.

'Smelly toads,' he whispered to the guard.

The branches parted. Henry climbed in.

'Did you attack them?' said Peter.

'Of course,' said Henry. 'Didn't you hear Margaret screaming?'

'I was the one who heard their password, so I think I should have gone,' said Peter.

'Whose club is this?' said Henry.

The corners of Peter's mouth began to turn down.

'Right, out!' said Henry.

'Sorry!' said Peter. 'Please, Henry, can I be a real member of the Purple Hand?'

'No,' said Henry. 'You're too young. And don't you dare come into the fort when I'm not here.'

'I won't,' said Peter.

'Good,' said Henry. 'Now here's the plan. I'm going to set a booby trap in Margaret's tent. Then when she goes in . . .' Henry shrieked with laughter as he pictured Moody Margaret covered in cold muddy water.

All was not well back at Moody Margaret's Secret Club.

'It's your fault,' said Margaret.

'It isn't,' said Susan.

'You're such a blabbermouth, and you're a terrible spy.'

'I am not,' said Susan.

'Well, I'm Leader, and I ban you from the club for a week for breaking our sacred rule and telling the enemy our password. Now go away.'

'Oh please let me stay,' said Susan.

'No,' said Margaret.

Susan knew there was no point arguing with Margaret when she got that horrible bossy look on her face.

'You're so mean,' said Susan.

Moody Margaret picked up a book and started to read.

Sour Susan got up and left.

'I know what I'll do to fix Henry,' thought Margaret. 'I'll set a booby trap in Henry's fort. Then when he goes in . . .' Margaret shrieked with laughter as she pictured Horrid Henry covered in cold muddy water.

Just before lunch Henry sneaked into Margaret's garden holding a plastic bucket of water and some string. He stretched the string just above the ground across the entrance and suspended the bucket above, with the other end of the string tied round it.

Just after lunch Margaret sneaked into Henry's garden holding a bucket of water and some string. She stretched the string across the fort's entrance and rigged up the bucket. What she wouldn't give to see Henry soaking wet when he tripped over the string and pulled the bucket of water down on him.

Perfect Peter came into the garden carrying a ball. Henry wouldn't play with him and there was nothing to do.

Why shouldn't I go into the fort? thought Peter. I helped build it.

Next door, Sour Susan slipped into the garden. She was feeling sulky.

Why shouldn't I go into the tent? thought Susan. It's my club too.

Perfect Peter walked into the fort and tripped. CRASH! SPLASH!

Sour Susan walked into the tent and tripped. CRASH! SPLASH!

Horrid Henry heard howls. He ran into the garden whooping.

'Ha! Ha! Margaret! Gotcha!'

Then he stopped.

Moody Margaret heard screams. She ran into the garden cheering.

'Ha! Ha! Henry! Gotcha!'

Then she stopped.

'That's it!' shrieked Peter. 'I'm leaving!'

'But it wasn't me,' said Henry.

'That's it!' sobbed Susan. 'I quit!'

'But it wasn't me,' said Margaret.

'Rats!' said Henry.

'Rats!' said Margaret.

They glared at each other.

EVIL ENEMY

Sour Susan

HFHZMSZH KLMTB KZMGH.

PURPLE HAND FORT

RULES

No girls allowed
Henry: Leader
Ralph: Deputy Leader.
Peter: Sentry (junior)
Henry's Title: Lord High Excellent Majesty
Peters Title: Worm

Peter must bow to Henry and Ralph
Peter must never touch the Purple hand Skull and
        Crossbones biscuit tin
Peter not allowed in the PurpleHand Fort
        without Henry's permission
Peter is a tempory member only.
Password: Smelly Toads
Motto: Down with girls

SECRET CLUB

Rules

No boys allowed
Margaret: Leader
Susan: Spy
Gurinder: biscuits and trainee spy
Linda: biscuits

Password: Nunga
Motto: Down with boys

Perfect Peter sat on the sofa looking through the Toy Heaven catalogue. Henry had hogged it all morning to write his Christmas present list. Naturally, this was not a list of the presents Henry planned to give. This was a list of what he wanted to get.

Horrid Henry looked up from his work. He'd got a bit stuck after: a million pounds, a parrot, a machete, swimming pool, trampoline, and Killer Catapult.

'Gimme that!' shouted Horrid Henry. He snatched the Toy Heaven catalogue from Perfect Peter.

'You give that back!' shouted Peter.

'It's my turn!' shouted Henry.

'You've had it the whole morning!' shrieked Peter. 'Mum!'

'Stop being horrid, Henry,' said Mum, running in from the kitchen.

Henry ignored her. His eyes were glued to the catalogue. He'd found it. The toy of his dreams. The toy he had to have.

'I want a Boom–Boom Basher,' said Henry. It was a brilliant toy which crashed into everything, an ear-piercing siren wailing all the while. Plus all the trasher attachments. Just the thing for knocking down Perfect Peter's marble run.

'I've got to have a Boom–Boom Basher,' said Henry, adding it to his list in big letters.

'Absolutely not, Henry,' said Mum. 'I will not have that horrible noisy toy in my house.'

'Aw, come on,' said Henry. 'Pleeease.'

Dad came in.

'I want a Boom-Boom Basher for Christmas,' said Henry.

'No way,' said Dad. 'Too expensive.'

'You are the meanest, most horrible parents in the whole world,' screamed Henry. 'I hate you! I want a Boom-Boom Basher!'

'That's no way to ask, Henry,' said Perfect Peter. 'I want doesn't get.'

Henry lunged at Peter. He was an octopus squeezing the life out of the helpless fish trapped in its tentacles.

'Help,' spluttered Peter.

'Stop being horrid, Henry, or I'll cancel the visit to Father Christmas,' shouted Mum.

Henry stopped.

The smell of burning mince pies drifted into the room.

'Ahh, my pies!' shrieked Mum.

41

'How much longer are we going to have to wait?' whined Henry. 'I'm sick of this!'

Horrid Henry, Perfect Peter, and Mum were standing near the end of a very long queue waiting to see Father Christmas. They had been waiting for a very long time.

'Oh, Henry, isn't this exciting,' said Peter. 'A chance to meet Father Christmas. I don't mind how long I wait.'

'Well I do,' snapped Henry. He began to squirm his way through the crowd.

'Hey, stop pushing!' shouted Dizzy Dave.

'Wait your turn!' shouted Moody Margaret.

'I was here first!' shouted Lazy Linda.

Henry shoved his way in beside Rude Ralph.

'What are you asking Father Christmas for?' said Henry. 'I want a Boom-Boom Basher.'

'Me too,' said Ralph. 'And a Goo-Shooter.'

Henry's ears pricked up.

'What's that?'

'It's really cool,' said Ralph. 'It splatters green goo over everything and everybody.'

'Yeah!' said Horrid Henry as Mum dragged him back to his former place in the queue.

'What do you want for Christmas, Graham?' asked Santa.

'Sweets!' said Greedy Graham.

'What do you want for Christmas, Bert?' asked Santa.

'I dunno,' said Beefy Bert.

'What do you want for Christmas, Peter?' asked Santa.

'A dictionary!' said Peter. 'Stamps, seeds, a geometry kit, and some cello music, please.'

'No toys?'

'No thank you,' said Peter. 'I have plenty of toys already. Here's a present for you, Santa,' he added, holding out a beautifully wrapped package. 'I made it myself.'

'What a delightful young man,' said Santa. Mum beamed proudly.

'My turn now,' said Henry, pushing Peter off Santa's lap.

'And what do you want for Christmas, Henry?' asked Santa.

Henry unrolled the list.

'I want a Boom–Boom Basher and a Goo-Shooter,' said Henry.

'Well, we'll see about that,' said Santa.

'Great!' said Henry. When grown-ups said 'We'll see,' that almost always meant 'Yes.'

It was Christmas Eve.

Mum and Dad were rushing around the house tidying up as fast as they could.

Perfect Peter was watching a nature programme on TV.

'I want to watch cartoons!' said Henry. He grabbed the clicker and switched channels.

'I was watching the nature programme!' said Peter. 'Mum!'

'Stop it, Henry,' muttered Dad. 'Now, both of you, help tidy up before your aunt and cousin arrive.'

Perfect Peter jumped up to help.

Horrid Henry didn't move.

'Do they have to come?' said Henry.

'Yes,' said Mum.

'I hate cousin Steve,' said Henry.

'No you don't,' said Mum.

'I do too,' snarled Henry. If there was a yuckier person walking the earth than Stuck-up Steve, Henry had yet to meet him. It was the one bad thing about Christmas, having him come to stay every year.

Ding Dong. It must be Rich Aunt Ruby and his horrible cousin. Henry watched as his aunt staggered in carrying boxes and boxes of presents which she dropped under the brightly-lit tree. Most of them, no doubt, for Stuck-up Steve.

'I wish we weren't here,' moaned Stuck-up Steve.
'Our house is so much nicer.'

'Shh,' said Rich Aunt Ruby. She went off with
Henry's parents.

Stuck-up Steve looked down at Henry.

'Bet I'll get loads more presents than you,' he said.

'Bet you won't,' said Henry, trying to sound
convinced.

'It's not what you get it's the thought that counts,'
said Perfect Peter.

'*I'm* getting a Boom-Boom Basher *and* a Goo-
Shooter,' said Stuck-up Steve.

'So am I,' said Henry.

'Nah,' said Steve. 'You'll just get horrible
presents like socks and stuff. And won't I laugh.'

When I'm king, thought Henry, I'll have a snake pit

made just for Steve.

'I'm richer than you,' boasted Steve. 'And I've got loads more toys.' He looked at the Christmas tree.

'Call that twig a tree?' sneered Steve. 'Ours is so big it touches the ceiling.'

'Bedtime, boys,' called Dad. 'And remember, no one is to open any presents until we've eaten lunch and gone for a walk.'

'Good idea, Dad,' said Perfect Peter. 'It's always nice to have some fresh air on Christmas Day and leave the presents for later.'

Ha, thought Horrid Henry. We'll see about that.

The house was dark. The only noise was the rasping sound of Stuck-up Steve, snoring away in his sleeping bag.

Horrid Henry could not sleep. Was there a Boom-Boom Basher waiting for him downstairs?

He rolled over on his side and tried to get comfortable. It was no use. How could he live until Christmas morning?

Horrid Henry could bear it no longer. He had to find out if he'd been given a Boom-Boom Basher.

Henry crept out of bed, grabbed his torch, stepped over Stuck-up Steve – resisting the urge to stomp on him – and sneaked down the stairs.

CR-EEAK went the creaky stair. Henry froze. The house was silent.

Henry tiptoed into the dark sitting room. There was the tree. And there were all the presents, loads and

48

loads and loads of them!

Right, thought Henry, I'll just have a quick look for my Boom-Boom Basher and then get straight back to bed.

He seized a giant package. This looked promising. He gave it a shake. Thud-thud-thunk. This sounds good, thought Henry. His heart leapt. I just know it's a Boom-Boom Basher. Then he checked the label: 'Merry Christmas, Steve.'

Rats, thought Henry.

He shook another temptingly-shaped present: 'Merry Christmas, Steve.' And another: 'Merry Christmas, Steve.' And another. And another.

Then Henry felt a small, soft, squishy package. Socks for sure. I hope it's not for me, he thought. He checked the label: 'Merry Christmas, Henry.'

There must be some mistake, thought Henry. Steve needs socks more than I do. In fact, I'd be doing him a favour giving them to him.

Switch! It was the work of a moment to swap labels.

Now, let's see, thought Henry. He eyed a Goo-Shooter shaped package with Steve's name on it, then found another, definitely book-shaped one, intended for himself.

Switch!

Come to think of it, Steve had far too many toys

cluttering up his house. Henry had heard Aunt Ruby complaining about the mess just tonight.

Switch! Switch! Switch! Then Horrid Henry crept back to bed.

It was 6:00 a.m.

'Merry Christmas!' shouted Henry. 'Time to open the presents!'

Before anyone could stop him Henry thundered downstairs.

Stuck-up Steve jumped up and followed him.

'Wait!' shouted Mum.

'Wait!' shouted Dad.

The boys dashed into the sitting room and flung themselves upon the presents. The room was filled with shrieks of delight and howls of dismay as they tore off the wrapping paper.

'Socks!' screamed Stuck-up Steve. 'What a crummy present! Thanks for nothing!'

'Don't be so rude, Steve,' said Rich Aunt Ruby, yawning.

'A Goo-Shooter!' shouted Horrid Henry. 'Wow! Just what I wanted!'

'A geometry set,' said Perfect Peter. 'Great!'

'A flower-growing kit?' howled Stuck-up Steve. 'Phooey!'

'Make Your Own Fireworks!' beamed Henry. 'Wow!'

'Tangerines!' screamed Stuck-up Steve. 'This is the worst Christmas ever!'

'A Boom-Boom Basher!' beamed Henry. 'Gee, thanks. Just what I wanted!'

'Let me see that label,' snarled Steve. He grabbed
the torn wrapping paper. 'Merry Christmas, Henry,'
read the label. There was no mistake.

'Where's *my* Boom-Boom Basher?' screamed Steve.

'It must be here somewhere,' said Aunt Ruby.

'Ruby, you shouldn't have bought one for Henry,'
said Mum, frowning.

'I didn't,' said Ruby.

Mum looked at Dad.

'Nor me,' said Dad.

'Nor me,' said Mum.

'Father Christmas gave it to me,' said Horrid Henry. 'I asked him to and he did.'

Silence.

'He's got my presents!' screamed Steve. 'I want them back!'

'They're mine!' screamed Henry, clutching his booty. 'Father Christmas gave them to me.'

'No, mine!' screamed Steve.

Aunt Ruby inspected the labels. Then she looked grimly at the two howling boys.

'Perhaps I made a mistake when I labelled some of the presents,' she muttered to Mum. 'Never mind. We'll sort it out later,' she said to Steve.

'It's not fair!' howled Steve.

'Why don't you try on your new socks?' said Horrid Henry.

Stuck-up Steve lunged at Henry. But Henry was ready for him.

SPLAT!

'Aaaarggh!' screamed Steve, green goo dripping from his face and clothes and hair.

'HENRY!' screamed Mum and Dad. 'How could you be so horrid!'

'Boom-Boom

CRASH!
NEE NAW NEE NAW
WHOO WHOOO WHOOO!'

What a great Christmas, thought Henry, as his Boom-Boom Basher knocked over Peter's marble run.

'Say goodbye to Aunt Ruby, Henry,' said Mum. She looked tired.

Rich Aunt Ruby and Steve had decided to leave a little earlier than planned.

'Goodbye, Aunt,' said Henry. 'Goodbye, Steve. Can't wait to see you next Christmas.'

'Actually,' said Mum, 'you're staying the night next month.'

Uh-oh, thought Horrid Henry.

EVIL ENEMY

Stuck-up
Steve

R DZMG Z PROOVI XZGZKFOG
ZMW YLLN-YLLN YZHSVI.

Dear Henry
Thank you for the socks and
tangerines (not)
                    Steve.

P.S. My mum made me write this.

Dear Steve
Wow! Thank you so
        MUCH
for the Boom-Boom Basher
and Goo Shooter!
I think of you every time
I play with them!!!
What GREAT presents!
Hard luck you got socks.
                    Henry

Margaret, you old pants face!
How dare you booby trap my fort!!!
You are dead meat — the Purple Hand will get you!
The Purple Hand

HORRID HENRY'S HAUNTED HOUSE

'**N**o way!' shrieked Horrid Henry. He was not staying the weekend with his slimy cousin Stuck-up Steve, and that was that. He sat in the back seat of the car with his arms folded.

'Yes you are,' said Mum.

'Steve can't wait to see you,' said Dad.

This was not exactly true. After Henry had sprayed Steve with green goo last Christmas, *and* helped himself to a few of Steve's presents, Steve had sworn revenge. Under the circumstances, Henry thought it would be a good idea to keep out of Steve's way.

And now Mum had arranged for him to spend the weekend while she and Dad went off on their own! Perfect Peter was staying with Tidy Ted, and he was stuck with Steve.

'It's a great chance for you boys to become good friends,' she said. 'Steve is a very nice boy.'

'I feel sick,' said Henry, coughing.

'Stop faking,' said Mum. 'You were well enough to play football all morning.'

'I'm too tired,' said Henry, yawning.

'I'm sure you'll get plenty of rest at Aunt Ruby's,' said Dad firmly.

'I'M NOT GOING!' howled Henry.

Mum and Dad took Henry by the arms, dragged him to Rich Aunt Ruby's door, and rang the bell.

The massive door opened immediately.

'Welcome, Henry,' said Rich Aunt Ruby, giving him a great smacking kiss.

'Henry, how lovely to see you,' said Stuck-up Steve sweetly. 'That's a very nice second-hand jumper you're wearing.'

'Hush, Steve,' said Rich Aunt Ruby. 'I think Henry looks very smart.'

Henry glared at Steve. Thank goodness he'd remembered his Goo-Shooter. He had a feeling he might need it.

'Goodbye, Henry,' said Mum. 'Be good. Ruby, thank you so much for having him.'

'Our pleasure,' lied Aunt Ruby.

The great door closed.

Henry was alone in the house with his arch-enemy.

Henry looked grimly at Steve. What a horrible boy, he thought.

Steve looked grimly at Henry. What a horrible boy, he thought.

'Why don't you both go upstairs and play in Steve's room till supper's ready?' said Aunt Ruby.

'I'll show Henry where he's sleeping first,' said Steve.

'Good idea,' said Aunt Ruby.

Reluctantly, Henry followed his cousin up the wide staircase.

'I bet you're scared of the dark,' said Steve.

''Course I'm not,' said Henry.

'That's good,' said Steve. 'This is my room,' he added, opening the door to an enormous bedroom. Horrid Henry stared longingly at the shelves filled to bursting with zillions of toys and games.

'Of course all *my* toys are brand new. Don't you dare touch anything,' hissed Steve. 'They're all mine and only *I* can play with them.'

Henry scowled. When he was king he'd use Steve's head for target practice.

They continued all the way to the top. Goodness, this old house was big, thought Henry.

Steve opened the door to a large attic bedroom, with brand new pink and blue flowered wallpaper, a four-poster bed, an enormous polished wood wardrobe, and two large windows.

'You're in the haunted room,' said Steve casually.

'Great!' said Henry. 'I love ghosts.' It would take more than a silly ghost to frighten *him*.

'Don't believe me if you don't want to,' said Steve. 'Just don't blame me when the ghost starts wailing.'

'You're nothing but a big fat liar,' said Henry. He

was sure Steve was lying. He was absolutely sure Steve was lying. He was one million percent sure that Steve was lying.

He's just trying to pay me back for Christmas, thought Henry.

Steve shrugged. 'Suit yourself. See that stain on the carpet?'

Henry looked down at something brownish.

'That's where the ghost vaporized,' whispered Steve. 'Of course if you're too scared to sleep here . . .'

Henry would rather have walked on hot coals than admit being scared to Steve.

He yawned, as if he'd never heard anything so boring.

'I'm looking forward to meeting the ghost,' said Henry.

'Good,' said Steve.

'Supper, boys!' called Aunt Ruby.

Henry lay in bed. Somehow he'd survived the dreadful meal and Stuck-up Steve's bragging about his expensive clothes, toys and trainers. Now here he was, alone in the attic at the top of the house. He'd jumped into bed, carefully avoiding the faded brown patch on the floor. He was sure it was just spilled cola or some-thing, but just in case . . .

Henry looked around him. The only thing he didn't like was the huge wardrobe opposite the bed. It loomed

up in the darkness at him. You could hide a body in that wardrobe, thought Henry, then rather wished he hadn't.

'Ooooooooooh.'

Henry stiffened.

Had he just imagined the sound of someone moaning?

Silence.

Nothing, thought Henry, snuggling down under the covers. Just the wind.

'Ooooooooooh.'

This time the moaning was a fraction louder. The hairs on Henry's neck stood up. He gripped the sheets tightly.

'Haaaaaahhhhhhh.'

Henry sat up.

'Haaaaaaaaahhhhhhhhhhh.'

The ghostly breathy moaning sound was not coming from outside. It appeared to be coming from inside the giant wardrobe.

Quickly, Henry switched on the bedside light.

What am I going to do? thought Henry. He wanted to run screaming to his aunt.

But the truth was, Henry was too frightened to move.

Some dreadful moaning thing was inside the wardrobe.

Just waiting to get *him*.

And then Horrid Henry remembered who he was. Leader of a pirate gang. Afraid of nothing (except injections).

I'll just get up and check inside that wardrobe, he thought. Am I a man or a mouse?

Mouse! he thought.

He did not move.

'Ooooooooaaaaahhhhhh,' moaned the THING. The unearthly noises were getting louder.

Shall I wait here for IT to get me, or shall I make a move first? thought Henry. Silently, he reached under the bed for his Goo-Shooter.

Then slowly, he swung his feet over the bed.

Holding his breath, Horrid Henry stood outside the wardrobe.

'HAHAHAHAHAHAHAHHA!'

Henry jumped. Then he flung open the door and fired.

SPLAT!

'HAHAHAHAHAHAHAHAHAHAHAHA ughhhhhhh –'

The wardrobe was empty.

Except for something small and greeny-black on the top shelf.

It looked like – it was!

Henry reached up and took it.

It was a cassette player. Covered in green goo.

Inside was a tape. It was called 'Dr Jekyll's Spooky Sounds.'

Steve, thought Horrid Henry grimly. REVENGE!

'Did you sleep well, dear?' asked Aunt Ruby at breakfast.

'Like a log,' said Henry.

'No strange noises?' asked Steve.

'No,' smiled Henry sweetly. 'Why, did you hear something?'

Steve looked disappointed. Horrid Henry kept his face blank. He couldn't wait for the evening.

Horrid Henry spent a busy day.

He went ice-skating.

He went to the cinema.

He played football.

After supper, Henry went straight to bed.

'It's been a lovely day,' he said. 'But I'm tired. Goodnight, Aunt Ruby. Goodnight, Steve.'

'Goodnight, Henry,' said Ruby.

Steve ignored him.

But Henry did not go to his bedroom. Instead he sneaked into Steve's.

He wriggled under Steve's bed and lay there, waiting.

Soon Steve came into the room. Henry resisted the urge to reach out and seize Steve's skinny leg. He had something much scarier in mind.

He heard Steve putting on his blue bunny pyjamas and jumping into bed. Henry waited until the room was dark.

Steve lay above him, humming to himself.

'Dooby dooby dooby do,' sang Steve.

Slowly, Henry reached up, and ever so slightly, poked the mattress.

Silence.

'Dooby dooby dooby do,' sang Steve, a little more quietly.

Henry reached up and poked the mattress again.

Steve sat up.

Then he lay back.

Henry poked the mattress again, ever so slightly.

'Must be my imagination,' muttered Steve.

Henry allowed several moments to pass. Then he twitched the duvet.

'Mummy,' whimpered Steve.

Jab! Henry gave the mattress a definite poke.

'AHHHHHHHHHHHH!' screamed Steve. He leaped up and ran out of the room. 'MUMMY! HELP! MONSTERS!'

Henry scrambled out of the room and ran silently up to his attic. Quick as he could he put on his pyjamas, then clattered noisily back down the stairs to Steve's.

Aunt Ruby was on her hands and knees, peering under the bed. Steve was shivering and quivering in the corner.

'There's nothing here, Steve,' she said firmly.

'What's wrong?' asked Henry.

'Nothing,' muttered Steve.

'You're not *scared* of the dark, are you?' said Henry.

'Back to bed, boys,' said Aunt Ruby. She left the room.

'Ahhhhh, Mummy, help! Monsters!' mimicked Henry, sticking out his tongue.

'MUM!' wailed Steve. 'Henry's being horrid!'

'GO TO BED, BOTH OF YOU!' shrieked Ruby.

'Watch out for monsters,' said Henry.

Steve did not move from his corner.

'Want to swap rooms tonight?' said Henry.

Steve did not wait to be asked twice.

'Oh yes,' said Steve.

'Go on up,' said Henry. 'Sweet dreams.'

Steve dashed out of his bedroom as fast as he could.

Tee hee, thought Horrid Henry, pulling Steve's toys down from the shelves. Now, what would he play with first?

Oh, yes. He'd left a few spooky sounds of his own under the attic bed – just in case.

KVG VI RH Z HNVOOB GLZW DLIN.

NRHH YZGGOV-ZCV VZGH MRGH.

BEWARE!! EVIL GROWN-UPS!

Nurse Needle
Most evil crime: giving me an injection

Soggy Sid
Most evil crime: ordering me into the pool

Impatience Tutu
Most evil crime: making me be a raindrop

Ninius Nerdon
Most evil crime: thinking he could beat me

Boudicca Battle-Axe
Most evil crime: being my teacher

Prissy Polly
Most evil crime: forcing me to be a page boy

Pimply Paul
Most evil crime: marrying Prissy Polly

Greasy Greta the Demon Dinner Lady
Most evil crime: nicking my crisps

Fat chance Henry
You're no match for us.
Beware the full moon.
The Secret Club rules

MOODY MARGARET MOVES IN

Mum was on the phone.

'Of course we'd be delighted to have Margaret,' she said. 'It will be no trouble at all.'

Henry stopped breaking the tails off Peter's plastic horses.

'WHAT?' he howled.

'Shh, Henry,' said Mum. 'No, no,' she added. 'Henry is delighted, too. See you Friday.'

'What's going on?' said Henry.

'Margaret is coming to stay while her parents go on holiday,' said Mum.

Henry was speechless with horror.

'She's going to stay . . . here?'

'Yes,' said Mum.

'How long?' said Henry.

'Two weeks,' said Mum brightly.

Horrid Henry could not stand Moody Margaret for more than two minutes.

'Two weeks?' he said. 'I'll run away! I'll lock her out of the house, I'll pull her hair out, I'll . . .'

'Don't be horrid, Henry,' said Mum. 'Margaret's a lovely girl and I'm sure we'll have fun.'

'No we won't,' said Henry. 'Not with that moody old grouch.'

'I'll have fun,' said Perfect Peter. 'I love having guests.'

78

'She's not sleeping in my room,' said Horrid Henry. 'She can sleep in the cellar.'

'No,' said Mum. 'You'll move into Peter's room and let Margaret have your bed.'

Horrid Henry opened his mouth to scream, but only a rasping sound came out. He was so appalled he could only gasp.

'Give . . . up . . . my . . . room!' he choked. 'To . . . Margaret?'

Margaret spying on *his* treasures, sleeping in *his* bed, playing with *his* toys while he had to share a room with Peter . . .

'No!' howled Henry. He fell on the floor and screamed. 'NO!!'

'I don't mind giving up my bed for a guest,' said Perfect Peter. 'It's the polite thing to do. Guests come first.'

Henry stopped howling just long enough to kick Peter.

'Owww!' screamed Peter. He burst into tears, 'Mum!'

'Henry!' yelled Mum. 'You horrid boy! Say sorry to Peter.'

'She's not coming!' shrieked Henry. 'And that's final.'

'Go to your room!' yelled Mum.

Moody Margaret arrived at Henry's house with her
parents, four suitcases, seven boxes of toys, two pillows,
and a trumpet.

'Margaret won't be any trouble,' said her mum.
'She's always polite, eats everything, and never
complains. Isn't that right, precious?'

'Yes,' said Margaret.

'Margaret's no fusspot,' said her dad. 'She's good as
gold, aren't you, precious?'

'Yes,' said Margaret.

'Have a lovely holiday,' said Mum.

'We will,' said Margaret's parents.

The door slammed behind them.

Moody Margaret marched into the sitting room and swept a finger across the mantelpiece.

'It's not very clean, is it?' she said. 'You'd never find so much dust at *my* house.'

'Oh,' said Dad.

'A little dust never hurt anyone,' said Mum.

'I'm allergic,' said Margaret. 'One whiff of dust and I start to . . . sn

. . . sn . . .

ACHOOO!'

she sneezed.

'We'll clean up right away,' said Mum.

Dad mopped.

Mum swept.

Peter dusted.

Henry hoovered.

Margaret directed.

'Henry, you've missed a big dust-ball right there,' said Margaret, pointing under the sofa.

Horrid Henry hoovered as far away from the dust as possible.

'Not there, here!' said Margaret.

Henry aimed the hoover at Margaret. He was a
fire-breathing dragon burning his prey to a crisp.

'Help!' shrieked Margaret.

'Henry!' said Dad.

'Don't be horrid,' said Mum.

'I think Henry should be punished,' said Margaret.
'I think he should be locked in his bedroom for three
weeks.'

'I don't have a bedroom to be locked up in 'cause
you're in it,' said Henry. He glared at Margaret.

Margaret glared back.

'I'm the guest, Henry, so you'd better be polite,'
hissed Margaret.

'Of course he'll be polite,' said Mum. 'Don't worry, Margaret. Any trouble, you come straight to me.'

'Thank you,' said Moody Margaret, smiling. 'I will. I'm hungry,' she added. 'Why isn't supper ready?'

'It will be soon,' said Dad.

'But I *always* eat at six o'clock,' said Margaret, 'I want to eat NOW.'

'All right,' said Dad.

Horrid Henry and Moody Margaret dashed for the seat facing the garden. Margaret got there first.

Henry shoved her off. Then Margaret shoved him off. Thud. Henry landed on the floor.

'Ouch,' said Henry.

'Let the guest have the chair,' said Dad.

'But that's *my* chair,' said Henry. 'That's where I *always* sit.'

'Have my chair, Margaret,' said Perfect Peter. 'I don't mind.'

'I want to sit here,' said Moody Margaret. 'I'm the guest so *I* decide.'

Horrid Henry dragged himself around the table and sat next to Peter.

'OUCH!' shrieked Margaret. 'Henry kicked me!'

'No I didn't,' said Henry, outraged.

'Stop it, Henry,' said Mum. 'That's no way to treat a guest.'

Henry stuck out his tongue at Margaret. Moody Margaret stuck out her tongue even further, then stomped on his foot.

'OUCH!' shrieked Henry. 'Margaret kicked me!'

Moody Margaret gasped. 'Oh I'm ever so sorry, Henry,' she said sweetly. 'It was an accident. Silly me. I didn't mean to, really I didn't.'

Dad brought the food to the table.

'What's *that*?' asked Margaret.

'Baked beans, corn on the cob, and chicken,' said Dad.

'I don't like baked beans,' said Margaret. 'And I like my corn *off* the cob.'

Mum scraped the corn off the cob.

'No, put the corn on a separate plate!' shrieked Margaret. 'I don't like vegetables touching my meat.'

Dad got out the pirate plate, the duck plate, and the 'Happy birthday Peter' plate.

'I want the pirate plate,' said Margaret, snatching it.

'I want the pirate plate,' said Henry, snatching it back.

'I don't mind which plate I get,' said Perfect Peter. 'A plate's a plate.'

'No it isn't!' shouted Henry.

'I'm the guest,' shouted Margaret. 'I get to choose.'

'Give her the pirate plate, Henry,' said Dad.

'It's not fair,' said Henry, glaring at his plate decorated with little ducks.

'She's the guest,' said Mum.

'So?' said Henry. Wasn't there an ancient Greek who stretched all his guests on an iron bed if they were too short or lopped off their heads and feet if they were too long? That guy sure knew how to deal with horrible guests like Moody Margaret.

'Yuck,' said Margaret, spitting out a mouthful of chicken. 'You've put salt on it!'

'Only a little,' said Dad.

'I never eat salt,' said Moody Margaret. 'It's not good for me. And I always have peas at *my* house.'

'We'll get some tomorrow,' said Mum.

Peter lay asleep in the top bunk. Horrid Henry sat listening by the door. He'd scattered crumbs all over Margaret's bed. He couldn't wait to hear her scream.

But there wasn't a sound coming from Henry's room, where Margaret the invader lay. Henry couldn't understand it.

Sadly, he climbed into (oh, the shame of it) the *bottom* bunk. Then he screamed. His bed was filled with jam, crumbs, and something squishy squashy and horrible.

'Go to sleep, Henry!' shouted Dad.

That Margaret! He'd booby-trap the room, cut up her doll's clothes, paint her face purple . . . Henry smiled grimly. Oh yes, he'd fix Moody Margaret.

Mum and Dad sat in the sitting room watching TV.

Moody Margaret appeared on the stairs.

'I can't sleep with that noise,' she said.

Mum and Dad looked at each other.

'We are watching very quietly, dear,' said Mum.

'But I can't sleep if there's any noise in the house,' said Margaret. 'I have very sensitive ears.'

Mum turned off the TV and picked up her knitting needles.

Click click click.

Margaret reappeared.

'I can't sleep with that clicking noise,' she said.

'All right,' said Mum. She sighed a little.

'And it's cold in my bedroom,' said Moody Margaret.

Mum turned up the heat.

Margaret reappeared.

'Now it's too hot,' said Moody Margaret.

Dad turned down the heat.

'My room smells funny,' said Margaret.

'My bed is too hard,' said Margaret.

'My room is too stuffy,' said Margaret.

'My room is too light,' said Margaret.

'Goodnight, Margaret,' said Mum.

'How many more days is she staying?' said Dad.

Mum looked at the calendar.

'Only thirteen,' said Mum.

Dad hid his face in his hands.

'I don't know if I can live that long,' said Dad.

mm

TOOT A TOOT.

Mum blasted out of bed.

TOOT A TOOT. Dad blasted out of bed.

TOOT A TOOT. TOOT A TOOT. TOOT A TOOT TOOT TOOT. Henry and Peter blasted out of bed.

Margaret marched down the hall, playing her trumpet.

TOOT A TOOT. TOOT A TOOT. TOOT A TOOT TOOT TOOT TOOT.

'Margaret, would you mind playing your trumpet a little later?' said Dad, clutching his ears. 'It's six o'clock in the morning.'

'That's when I wake up,' said Margaret.

'Could you play a little more softly?' said Mum.

'But I have to practise,' said Moody Margaret.

The trumpet blared through the house.

TOOT TOOT TOOT.

Horrid Henry turned on his boom box.

BOOM BOOM BOOM.

90

Margaret played her trumpet louder.

TOOT! TOOT! TOOT!

Henry blasted his boom box as loud as he could.

BOOM! BOOM! BOOM!

'Henry!' shrieked Mum.

'Turn that down!' bellowed Dad.

'Quiet!' screamed Margaret. 'I can't practise with all this noise.' She put down her trumpet. 'And I'm hungry. Where's my breakfast?'

'We have breakfast at eight,' said Mum.

'But I want breakfast now,' said Margaret.

Mum had had enough.

'No,' said Mum firmly. 'We eat at eight.'

Margaret opened her mouth and screamed. No one could scream as long, or as loud, as Moody Margaret.

Her piercing screams echoed through the house.

'All right,' said Mum. She knew when she was beaten. 'We'll eat now.'

Henry's diary

Monday I put crumbs in Margaret's bed. She put jam, crusts and slugs in mine.

Tuesday Margaret found my secret biscuits and crisps and ate every single one.

Wednesday I can't play tapes at night because it disturbs grumpy-face Margaret.

Thursday I can't sing because it disturbs frog-face.

Friday I can't breathe because it disturbs misery-guts.

Saturday I can stand it No Longer

That night, when everyone was asleep, Horrid Henry crept into the sitting room and picked up the phone.

'I'd like to leave a message,' he whispered.

Bang bang bang bang bang.

Ding dong! Ding dong! Ding dong!

Henry sat up in bed.

Someone was banging on the front door and ringing the bell.

'Who could that be at this time of night?' yawned Mum.

Dad peeked through the window then opened the door.

'Where's my baby?' shouted Margaret's mum.

'Where's my baby?' shouted Margaret's dad.

'Upstairs,' said Mum. 'Where else?'

'What's happened to her?' shrieked Margaret's mum.

'We got here as quick as we could!' shrieked Margaret's dad.

Mum and Dad looked at each other. What was going on?

'She's fine,' said Mum.

Margaret's mum and dad looked at each other. What was going on?

'But the message said it was an emergency and to come at once,' said Margaret's mum.

'We cut short our holiday,' said Margaret's dad.

'What message?' said Mum.

'What's going on? I can't sleep with all this noise,' said Moody Margaret.

Margaret and her parents had gone home.

'What a terrible mix-up,' said Mum.

'Such a shame they cut short their holiday,' said Dad.

'Still . . .' said Mum. She looked at Dad.

'Hmmn,' said Dad.

'You don't think that Henry . . .' said Mum.

'Not even Henry could do something so horrid,' said Dad.

Mum frowned.

'Henry!' said Mum.

Henry continued sticking Peter's stamps together. 'Yeah?'

'Do you know anything about a message?'

'Me?' said Henry.

'You,' said Mum.

'No,' said Henry. 'It's a mystery.'

'That's a lie, Henry,' said Perfect Peter.

'Is not,' said Henry.

'Is too,' said Peter. 'I heard you on the phone.'

Henry lunged at Peter. He was a mad bull charging the matador.

'YOWWWWW,' shrieked Peter.

Henry stopped. He was in for it now. No pocket money for a year. No sweets for ten years. No TV ever.

Henry squared his shoulders and waited for his punishment.

Dad put his feet up.

'That was a terrible thing to do,' said Dad.

Mum turned on the TV.

'Go to your room,' said Mum.

Henry bounced upstairs. Your room. Sweeter words were never spoken.

Dear Henry, Peter and Parents,

I think you should know all the things that are wrong at your house so that you can do better next time.

1. Everyone should go to bed when I do at 8.30 pm and not make any noise.
2. Guests should always be given the pirate plate.
3. Guests should always decide where they sit at the table.
4. I am allergic to dust. Clean your house more or I won't come back.
5. My breakfast should be served when I wake up at 6.30 am and not one minute later.
6. If you break my egg yolk you must start again.
7. You cooked lots of things I don't like. You should have asked me first. No baked beans. No corn on the cob. No salt.
8. Henry must be locked in his room with bread and water while I am staying.
9. If I think of anything else I will tell you.

Margaret

P.S. Thank you for having me to stay.

WANTED
DEAD OR ALIVE
Worlds most horrible girl
Guilty of
attacking Henry's Purple Hand Fort
putting jam crusts and slugs in Henry's bed;
annoying him, and other crimes

Moody Margaret

NZITZIVG RH Z KLGZGL.

HORRID HENRY'S RAID

'**Y**ou're such a pig, Susan!'

'No I'm not! You're the pig!'

'You are!' squealed Moody Margaret.

'You are!' squealed Sour Susan.

'Oink!'

'Oink!'

All was not well at Moody Margaret's Secret Club.

Sour Susan and Moody Margaret glared at each other inside the Secret Club tent. Moody Margaret waved the empty biscuit tin in Susan's sour face.

'*Someone* ate all the biscuits,' said Moody Margaret. 'And it wasn't me.'

'Well, it wasn't me,' said Susan.

'Liar!'

'Liar!'

Margaret stuck out her tongue at Susan.

Susan stuck out her tongue at Margaret.

Margaret yanked Susan's hair.

'Oww! You horrible meanie!' shrieked Susan. 'I hate you.'

She yanked Margaret's hair.

'OWWW!' screeched Moody Margaret. 'How dare you?'

They scowled at each other.

'Wait a minute,' said Margaret. 'You don't think –'

Not a million miles away, sitting on a throne inside the Purple Hand fort hidden behind prickly branches, Horrid Henry wiped a few biscuit crumbs from his mouth and burped. Umm, boy, nothing beat the taste of an arch-enemy's biscuits.

The branches parted.

'Password!' hissed Horrid Henry.

'Smelly toads.'

'Enter,' said Henry.

The sentry entered and gave the secret handshake.

'Henry, why –' began Perfect Peter.

'Call me by my title, Worm!'

'Sorry, Henry – I mean Lord High Excellent Majesty of the Purple Hand.'

'That's better,' said Henry. He waved his hand and

pointed at the ground. 'Be seated, Worm.'

'Why am I Worm and you're Lord High Excellent Majesty?'

'Because I'm the Leader,' said Henry.

'I want a better title,' said Peter.

'All right,' said the Lord High Excellent Majesty, 'you can be Lord Worm.'

Peter considered.

'What about Lord High Worm?'

'OK,' said Henry. Then he froze.

'Worm! Footsteps!'

Perfect Peter peeked through the leaves.

'Enemies approaching!' he warned.

Pounding feet paused outside the entrance.

'Password!' said Horrid Henry.

'Dog poo breath,' said Margaret, bursting in. Sour Susan followed.

'That's not the password,' said Henry.

'You can't come in,' squeaked the sentry, a little late.

'You've been stealing the Secret Club biscuits,' said Moody Margaret.

'Yeah, Henry,' said Susan.

Horrid Henry stretched and yawned.

'Prove it.'

Moody Margaret pointed to all the crumbs lying on the dirt floor.

'Where did all these crumbs come from, then?'

'Biscuits,' said Henry.

'So you admit it!' shrieked Margaret.

'Purple Hand biscuits,' said Henry. He pointed to the Purple Hand skull and crossbones biscuit tin.

'Liar, liar, pants on fire,' said Margaret.

Horrid Henry fell to the floor and started rolling around.

'Ooh, ooh, my pants are on fire, I'm burning, call the fire brigade!' shouted Henry.

Perfect Peter dashed off.
'Mum!' he hollered.
'Henry's pants are on fire!'

Margaret and Susan made a hasty retreat.

Horrid Henry stopped rolling and howled with laughter.

'Ha ha ha ha ha – the Purple Hand rules!' he cackled.

'We'll get you for this, Henry,' said Margaret.

'Yeah, yeah,' said Henry.

'You didn't really steal their biscuits, did you Henry?' asked Lord High Worm the following day.

'As if,' said Horrid Henry. 'Now get back to your guard duty. Our enemies may be planning a revenge attack.'

'Why do I always have to be the guard?' said Peter. 'It's not fair.'

'Whose club is this?' said Henry fiercely.

Peter's lip began to tremble.

'Yours,' muttered Peter.

'So if you want to stay as a temporary

Down with boys

member, you have to do what I say,' said Henry.

'OK,' said Peter.

'And remember, one day, if you're very good, you'll be promoted from junior sentry to chief sentry,' said Henry.

'Ooh,' said Peter, brightening.

Business settled, Horrid Henry reached for the biscuit tin. He'd saved five yummy chocolate fudge chewies for today.

Henry picked up the tin and stopped. Why wasn't it rattling? He shook it.

Silence.

Horrid Henry ripped off the lid and shrieked.

The Purple Hand biscuit tin was empty. Except for one thing. A dagger drawn on a piece of paper. The dastardly mark of Margaret's Secret Club! Well, he'd show them who ruled.

'Worm!' he shrieked. 'Get in here!'

Peter entered.

'We've been raided!' screamed Henry. 'You're fired!'

'Waaaah!' wailed Peter.

'Good work, Susan,' said the Leader of the Secret
Club, her face covered in chocolate.

'I don't see why you got three biscuits and I only
got two when I was the one who sneaked in and stole
them,' said Susan sourly.

'Tribute to your Leader,' said Moody Margaret.

'I still don't think it's fair,' muttered Susan.

'Tough,' said Margaret. 'Now let's hear your spy
report.'

'NAH NAH NEE NAH NAH!' screeched a voice
from outside.

Susan and Margaret dashed out of the Secret Club
tent. They were too late. There was Henry, prancing
off, waving the Secret Club banner he'd stolen.

'Give that back, Henry!' screamed Margaret.

'Make me!' said Henry.

Susan chased him. Henry darted.
Margaret chased him. Henry dodged.
'Come and get me!' taunted Henry.

'All right,' said Margaret. She walked towards him, then suddenly jumped over the wall into Henry's garden and ran to the Purple Hand fort.

'Hey, get away from there!' shouted Henry, chasing after her. Where was that useless sentry when you needed him?

Margaret nabbed Henry's skull and crossbones flag, and darted off.

The two Leaders faced each other.

'Gimme my flag!' ordered Henry.

'Gimme my flag!' ordered Margaret.

'You first,' said Henry.

'*You* first,' said Margaret.

Neither moved.

'OK, at the count of three we'll throw them to each other,' said Margaret. 'One, two, three – throw!'

Margaret held on to Henry's flag.
Henry held on to Margaret's flag.
Several moments passed.
'Cheater,' said Margaret.
'Cheater,' said Henry.

'I don't know about you, but I have important spying work to get on with,' said Margaret.

'So?' said Henry. 'Get on with it. No one's stopping you.'

'Drop my flag, Henry,' said Margaret.

'No,' said Henry.

'Fine,' said Margaret. 'Susan! Bring me the scissors.'
Susan ran off.

'Peter!' shouted Henry. 'Worm! Lord Worm! Lord High Worm!'

Peter stuck his head out of the upstairs window.

'Peter! Fetch the scissors! Quick!'
ordered Henry.

'No,' said Peter. 'You fired me, remember?'
And he slammed the window shut.

'You're dead, Peter,' shouted Henry.

Sour Susan came back with the scissors and
gave them to Margaret. Margaret held the
scissors to Henry's flag. Henry didn't budge. She
wouldn't dare –

Snip!

Aaargh! Moody Margaret cut off a corner of
Henry's flag. She held the scissors poised to make
another cut.

Horrid Henry had spent hours painting his
beautiful flag. He knew when he was beaten.

'Stop!' shrieked Henry.

He dropped Margaret's flag. Margaret dropped his

flag. Slowly, they inched towards each other, then dashed to grab their own flag.

'Truce?' said Moody Margaret, beaming.

'Truce,' said Horrid Henry, scowling.

I'll get her for this, thought Horrid Henry. No one touches my flag and lives.

Horrid Henry watched and waited until it was dark and he heard the plinky-plonk sound of Moody Margaret practising her piano.

The coast was

clear. Horrid Henry sneaked outside, jumped over the wall and darted inside the Secret Club Tent.

Swoop! He swept up the Secret Club pencils and secret code book.

Snatch! He snaffled the Secret Club stool.

Grab! He bagged the Secret Club biscuit tin.

Was that everything?

No!

Scoop! He snatched the Secret Club motto ('Down with boys').

Pounce! He pinched the Secret Club carpet.

Horrid Henry looked around. The Secret Club tent was bare.

Except for –

Henry considered. Should he?

Yes!

Whisk! The Secret Club tent collapsed. Henry gathered it into his arms with the rest of his spoils.

Huffing and puffing, gasping and panting, Horrid Henry staggered off over the wall, laden with the Secret Club. Raiding was hot, heavy work, but a pirate had to do his duty. Wouldn't all this booty look great decorating his fort? A rug on the floor, an extra biscuit tin, a repainted motto – 'Down with girls' – yes, the Purple Hand Fort would have to be renamed the Purple Hand Palace.

Speaking of which, where was the Purple Hand Fort?

Horrid Henry looked about wildly for the Fort entrance.

It was gone.

He searched for the Purple Hand throne.

It was gone.

And the Purple Hand biscuit tin – GONE!

There was a rustling sound in the shadows. Horrid Henry turned and saw a strange sight.

There was the Purple Hand Fort leaning against the shed.

What?!

Suddenly the Fort started moving. Slowly, jerkily, the Fort wobbled across the lawn towards the wall on its four new stumpy legs.

Horrid Henry was livid. How dare someone try to nick his fort! This was an outrage. What was the world coming to, when people just sneaked into your garden and made off with your fort? Well, no way!

Horrid Henry let out a pirate roar.

'RAAAAAAAA!' roared Horrid Henry.

'AHHHHHHH!' shrieked the Fort.

CRASH!

The Purple Hand Fort fell to the ground. The raiders ran off, squabbling.

'I told you to hurry, you lazy lump!'

'You're the lazy lump!'

Victory!

Horrid Henry climbed to the top of his fort and grabbed his banner. Waving it proudly, he chanted his victory chant:

NAH NAH NE NAH NAH!

Catapult them
into a moat filled
with piranha fish

Let crocodiles
loose in their
bedrooms

Exile to an island
with no TV

ke them eat
hool dinners

How to Get Rid of EVIL ENEMIES

Dump them in snakepits

Drop them in vats of glop

BEWARE!! EVIL GROWN-UPS!

Nurse Needle

Rabid Rebecca

Miss Battle-Axe

Greasy Greta,
the Demon Dinner
lady

HORRID HENRY GOES TO WORK

'It's your turn!'

'No, it's yours!'

'Yours!'

'Yours!'

'I took Henry last year!' said Mum.

Dad paused. 'Are you sure?'

'YES,' said Mum.

'Are you sure you're sure?' said Dad. He looked pale.

'Of course I'm sure!' said Mum. 'How could I forget?'

Tomorrow was take your child to work day. Mum wanted to take Peter. Dad wanted to take Peter. Unfortunately, someone had to take Henry.

Only today Dad's boss had said how much he was looking forward to meeting Dad's lovely son. 'Of course I'll be bringing my boy, Bill,' said Big Boss. 'He's a great kid. Good as gold. Smart as a whip. Superb footballer. Brilliant at maths. Plays trumpet like a genius. Perfect manners. Yep, I sure am proud of Bill.'

Dad tried not to hate Bill. He failed.

'Now listen, Henry,' said Dad. 'You're coming to work with me tomorrow. I'm warning you, my boss is bringing *his* son. From what I hear he's perfect.'

'Like me?' said Peter. 'I'd love to meet him. We

could swap good deed ideas! Do you think he'd like to join my Best Boys Club?'

'You're going to Mum's work,' said Dad sadly. 'I'm taking Henry.'

'Cool!' said Henry. A day out of school! A day at the office! 'I want to play computer games. And eat doughnuts! And surf the web!'

'NO!' said Dad. 'An office is a place where people work. I want perfect behaviour. My boss is very strict. Don't let me down, Henry.'

'Of course I won't,' said Horrid Henry. He was outraged. How could Dad think such a thing? The only trouble was, how could Henry have any fun with a boring goody-goody like Bill around?

'Remember what I said, Henry,' said Dad the next morning, as they arrived at his office. 'Be nice to Bill. Do what he says. He's the boss's son. Try to be as good as he is.'

'All right,' said Henry sourly.

Dad's boss came to welcome them.

'Ah, you must be Henry!' said Big Boss. 'This is my son, Bill.'

'So pleased to meet you, Henry,' said Bossy Bill.

'Huh,' grunted Horrid Henry.

He looked at Bossy Bill. He was wearing a jacket and tie. His face was gleaming. His shoes were so polished Henry could see his dirty face in them. Just his luck to get stuck all day with boring old Bossy Bill.

'Right, boys, your first job is to make tea for everyone in the meeting room,' said Big Boss.

'Do I have to?' said Horrid Henry.

'Henry!' said Dad.

'Yes,' said Big Boss. 'That's six teas, one sugar in each.'

'Gee thanks, Dad!' said Bossy Bill. 'I love making tea.'

'Whoopee,' muttered Horrid Henry.

Big Boss beamed and left the room. Horrid Henry was alone with Bossy Bill.

The moment Big Boss left, Bill's face changed.

'Why doesn't he make his own stupid tea!' he snarled.

'I thought you loved making tea,' said Horrid Henry. Maybe things were looking up.

'No way,' said Bossy Bill. 'What am I, a servant? You make it.'

'You make it!' said Horrid Henry.

'You make it!' said Bossy Bill.

'No,' said Henry.

'Yes,' said Bill. 'It's my dad's company and you have to do what I say.'

'No I don't!' said Henry.

'Yes you do,' said Bill.

'I don't work for you,' said Henry.

'Yeah, but your dad works for *my* dad,' said Bossy Bill. 'If you don't do what I say I'll tell my dad to fire your dad.'

Horrid Henry glared at Bossy Bill, then slowly switched on the kettle. When he was king he'd build a shark tank specially for Bill.

Bossy Bill folded his arms and smirked as Henry poured hot water over the teabags. What a creep, thought Henry, licking his fingers and dipping them into the sugar bowl.

'You're disgusting,' said Bossy Bill. 'I'm telling on you.'

'Go ahead,' said Henry, licking sugar off his fingers. Next to his cousin Stuck-up Steve, Bossy Bill was the yuckiest kid he had ever met.

'Hey, I've got a great idea,' said Bill. 'Let's put salt in the tea instead of sugar.'

Horrid Henry hesitated. But hadn't Dad said to do what Bill told him?

'OK,' said Henry.

Bossy Bill poured a heaped teaspoon of salt into every cup.

'Now watch this,' said Bill.

'Thank you, Bill,' said Mr String. 'Aren't you clever!'

'Thank you, Bill,' said Ms Bean. 'Aren't you wonderful!'

'Thanks, Bill,' said Big Boss. 'How's the tea, everyone?'

'Delicious,' said Mr String. He put down the cup.

'Delightful,' said Ms Bean. She put down the cup.

'Umm,' said Dad. He put down the cup.

Then Big Boss took a sip. His face curdled.

'Disgusting!' he gasped, spitting out the tea. 'Bleeecch! Who put salt in this?'

'Henry did,' said Bill.

Horrid Henry was outraged.

'Liar!' said Henry. 'You did!'

'This tea is revolting,' said Mr String.

'Horrible,' said Ms Bean.

'I tried to stop him, Dad, but he just wouldn't

listen,' said Bossy Bill.

'I'm disappointed in you, Henry,' said Big Boss. 'Bill would never do anything like this.' He glanced at Dad. Dad looked as if he wished an alien spaceship would beam him up.

'But I didn't do it!' said Henry. He stared at Bill. What a creep!

'Now run along boys, and help answer the phones. Bill will show you how, Henry,' said Big Boss.

Horrid Henry followed Bill out of the meeting room. Beware, Bill, he thought. I'll get you for this.

Bill sat down at a huge desk and swung his feet up.

'Now copy me,' he said. 'Answer the phones just like I do.'

Ring ring.

'Hello, Elephant House!' said Bill.

Ring ring.

'Hello! Tootsie's Take-Away!' said Bill.

Ring ring.

'Hello! Pizza Parlour!' said Bill.

Ring ring.

'Go on, Henry, answer it.'

'No!' said Henry. After what had just happened with the tea, he'd never trust Bill again.

Ring ring.

'What are you, chicken?' said Bill.

'No,' said Henry.

'Then go on. *I* did it.'

Ring ring ring ring.

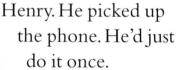

'All right,' said Henry. He picked up the phone. He'd just do it once.

'Hello Smelly! You're fired!'

Silence.

'Is that you, Henry?' said

125

Big Boss on the other end of the phone.

Eeek!

'Wrong number!' squeaked
Horrid Henry, and slammed down
the phone. Uh oh. Now he was in trouble. Big big
trouble.

Big Boss stormed into the room.

'What's going on in here?'

'I tried to stop him, but he just wouldn't listen,' said
Bossy Bill.

'That's not true!' squealed Horrid Henry. 'You
started it.'

'As if,' said Bossy Bill.

'And what have you been doing, son?' asked Big
Boss.

'Testing the phones for you,' said Bossy Bill. 'I think
there's a fault on line 2. I'll fix it in a minute.'

'That's my little genius,' beamed Big Boss.
He glared at Henry. Henry glared back.

'I told you to follow Bill's example!'
hissed Dad.

'I did!' hissed Henry.

Bossy Bill and Big Boss exchanged pitying glances.

'He's not usually like this,' lied Dad. He looked as if
he wished a whirlwind would whisk him away.

'I am usually like this!' said Henry. 'Just not today!'

'No pocket money for a year if there's any more

trouble,' muttered Dad.

This was so unfair. Why should he get blamed when it was absolutely definitely not his fault?

'I'll give you one more chance,' said Big Boss. He handed Henry a stack of papers. 'Photocopy these for the meeting this afternoon,' he said. 'If there are any more problems I will ask your father to take you home.'

Take him home! Dad would never ever forgive him. He was mad enough at Henry already. And it was all Bill's fault.

Scowling, Horrid Henry followed Bill into the photocopy room.

'Ha ha ha ha ha, I got you into trouble!' chortled Bill.

Horrid Henry resisted the urge to mash Bossy Bill into tiny bite-sized chunks. Instead, Horrid Henry started to think. Even if he was good as gold all day it would mean Bill had won. He had to come up with a plan to get back at Bill. Fast. But what? Anything awful Bill did Henry was sure to get the blame. No one would believe Henry hadn't done it. If his plan was to work, Bill had to be caught red-handed.

And then Horrid Henry had it. A perfectly brilliant, spectacularly evil plan. A plan to end all plans. A plan to go down in history. A plan – but there was no time to lose congratulating himself.

Bossy Bill snatched the papers from Henry's hand.

'I get to do the photocopying because it's *my* dad's office,' he said. 'If you're good I might let you hand out the papers.'

'Whatever you say,' said Horrid Henry humbly. 'After all, you're the boss.'

'Too right I am,' said Bossy Bill. 'Everyone has to do what I say.'

'Of course,' said Horrid Henry agreeably. 'Hey, I've got a great idea,' he added after a moment, 'why don't we make horrid faces, photocopy them and hang the pictures all round the meeting room?'

Bossy Bill's eyes gleamed.

'Yeah!' he said. He stuck out his tongue. He made a monkey face. He twisted his lips. 'Heh heh heh.' Then he paused. 'Wait a minute. We'd be recognised.'

Aaargh! Horrid Henry hadn't thought of that. His beautiful plan crumpled before him. Bill would win. Henry would lose. The terrible image of Bossy Bill laughing at him from here to eternity loomed before him. NO! No one ever tricked Horrid Henry and lived. I need a change of plan, thought Henry desperately. And then he knew what had to be done. It was risky. It was dangerous. But it was the only way.

'I know,' said Horrid Henry. 'Let's photocopy our bottoms instead.'

'Yeah!' said Bossy Bill. 'I was just going to suggest that.'

'I get to go first,' said Horrid Henry, shoving Bill out of the way.

'No, I do!' said Bill, shoving him back.

YES! thought Horrid Henry, as Bill hopped onto the photocopier. '*You* can paste up the pictures in the meeting room.'

'Great!' said Henry. He could tell what Bill was thinking. He'd get his dad to come in while Henry was sellotaping pictures of bottoms around the meeting room.

'I'll just get the sellotape,' said Henry.

'You do that,' said Bossy Bill, as the photocopier whirred into life.

Horrid Henry ran down the hall into Big Boss's office.

'Come quick, Bill's in trouble!' said Horrid Henry.

Big Boss dropped the phone and raced down the hall after Henry.

'Hold on, Bill, Daddy's coming!' he shrieked, and burst into the photocopy room.

There was Bossy Bill, perched on the photocopier, his back to the door, singing merrily:

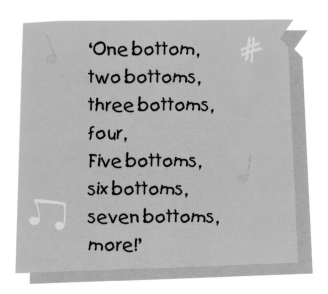

'One bottom,
two bottoms,
three bottoms,
four,
Five bottoms,
six bottoms,
seven bottoms,
more!'

'Bill!' screamed Big Boss.

'It was Henry!' screamed Bossy Bill. 'I was just testing the photocopier to make sure –'

'Be quiet, Bill!' shouted Big Boss. 'I saw what you were doing.'

'I tried to stop him but he just wouldn't listen,' said Horrid Henry.

Horrid Henry spent a lovely rest of the day at Dad's office. After Bill was grounded for a month and sent home in disgrace, Henry twirled all the chairs round and round. He sneaked up behind people and shouted, 'Boo!' Then he ate doughnuts, played computer games, and surfed the web. Boy, working in an office is fun, thought Horrid Henry. I'm going to enjoy getting a job when I grow up.

EVIL ENEMY

Bossy Bill

YROO SZH Z YRT SFT V TRMLI NLFH YLGGLN.

BATTLE PLANS

Sneak into Secret Club tent and **raid** biscuit tin while Margaret is practising her trumpet.

Spy on Secret Club meetings and foil all their evil plans.

Stinkbombs!

Boobytrap their club with a bucket of water over the entrance.

HORRID HENRY'S STINK BOMB

I hate you, Margaret!' shrieked Sour Susan. She stumbled out of the Secret Club tent.

'I hate you too!' shrieked Moody Margaret.

Sour Susan stuck out her tongue.

Moody Margaret stuck out hers back.

'I quit!' yelled Susan.

'You can't quit. You're fired!' yelled Margaret.

'You can't fire me. I quit!' said Susan.

'I fired you first,' said Margaret. 'And I'm changing the password!'

'Go ahead. See if I care. I don't want to be in the Secret Club any more!' said Susan sourly.

'Good! Because *we* don't want you.'

Moody Margaret flounced back inside the Secret Club tent. Sour Susan stalked off.

Free at last! Susan was sick and tired of her ex-best friend Bossyboots Margaret. Blaming *her* for the disastrous raid on the Purple Hand Fort when it was all Margaret's fault was bad enough. But then to ask stupid Linda to join the Secret Club without even telling her! Susan hated Linda even more than she hated Margaret. Linda hadn't invited

Ha ha Margaret,
You stink and so does
your pongy old club.
The Purple Hand

136

Susan to her sleepover party. And she was a copycat. But Margaret didn't care. Today she'd made Linda chief spy. Well, Susan had had enough. Margaret had been mean to her once too often.

Susan heard gales of laughter from inside the club tent. So they were laughing, were they? Laughing at her, no doubt? Well, she'd show them. She knew all about Margaret's Top Secret Plans. And she knew someone who would be very interested in that information.

'Halt! Password!'

'Smelly toads,' said Perfect Peter. He waited outside Henry's Purple Hand Fort.

'Wrong,' said Horrid Henry.

'What's the new one then?' said Perfect Peter.

'I'm not telling *you*,' said Henry. 'You're fired, remember?'

Perfect Peter did remember. He had hoped Henry had forgotten.

'Can't I join again, Henry?' asked Peter.

'No way!' said Horrid Henry.

'Please?' said Perfect Peter.

'No,' said Horrid Henry. 'Ralph's taken over your duties.'

Rude Ralph poked his head through the branches of Henry's lair.

'No babies allowed,' said Rude Ralph.

'We don't want you here, Peter,' said Horrid Henry. 'Get lost.'

Perfect Peter burst into tears.

'Crybaby!' jeered Horrid Henry.

'Crybaby!' jeered Rude Ralph.

That did it.

'Mum!' wailed Perfect Peter. He ran towards the house. 'Henry won't let me play and he called me a crybaby!'

'Stop being horrid, Henry!' shouted Mum.

Peter waited.

Mum didn't say anything else.

Perfect Peter started to wail louder.

'Muuum! Henry's being mean to me!'

'Leave Peter alone, Henry!' shouted Mum. She came out of the house. Her hands were covered in dough. 'Henry, if you don't stop –'

Mum looked around.

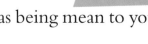

'Where's Henry?'

'In his fort,' snivelled Peter.

'I thought you said he was being mean to you,' said Mum.

'He was!' wailed Peter.

'Just keep away from him,' said Mum. She went back into the house.

Perfect Peter was outraged. Was that it? Why hadn't she punished Henry? Henry had been so horrid he deserved to go to prison for a year. Two years. And just get a crust of bread a week. And brussels sprouts. Ha! That would serve Henry right.

But until Henry went to prison, how could Peter pay him back?

And then Peter knew exactly what he could do.

He checked carefully to see that no one was watching. Then he sneaked over the garden wall and headed for the Secret Club Tent.

'He isn't!' said Margaret.

'She wouldn't,' said Henry.

'He's planning to swap our lemonade for a Dungeon Drink?' said Margaret.

'Yes,' said Peter.

She's planning to stinkbomb the Purple Hand Fort?' said Henry.

'Yes,' said Susan.

'How dare she?' said Henry.

'How dare he?' said Margaret. 'I'll easily put a stop to that. Linda!' she barked. 'Hide the lemonade!'

Linda yawned.

'Hide it yourself,' she said. 'I'm tired.'

Margaret glared at her, then hid the jug under a box.

'Ha ha! Won't Henry be shocked when he sneaks over and there are no drinks to spike!' gloated Margaret. 'Peter, you're a hero. I award you the Triple Star, the highest honour the Secret Club can bestow.'

'Ooh, thanks!' said Peter. It was nice being appreciated for a change.

'So from now on,' said Moody Margaret, 'you're working for me.'

'Okay,' said the traitor.

140

Horrid Henry rubbed his hands. This was fantastic! At last, he had a spy in the enemy's camp! He'd easily defend himself against that stupid stinkbomb. Margaret would only let it off when he was *in* the fort. His sentry would be on the lookout armed with a goo-shooter. When Margaret tried to sneak in with her stinkbomb — ker-pow!

'Hang on a sec,' said Horrid Henry, 'why should I trust you?'

'Because Margaret is mean and horrible and I hate her,' said Susan.

'So from now on,' said Horrid Henry, 'you're working for me.'

Susan wasn't sure she liked the sound of that. Then she remembered Margaret's mean cackle.

'Okay,' said the traitor.

Peter sneaked back into his garden and collided with someone.

'Ouch!' said Peter.

'Watch where you're going!' snapped Susan.

They glared at each other suspiciously.

'What were you doing at Margaret's?' said Susan.

'Nothing,' said Peter. 'What were you doing at my house?'

'Nothing,' said Susan.

Peter walked towards Henry's fort, whistling.

Susan walked towards Margaret's tent, whistling.

Well, if Susan was spying on Henry for Margaret, Peter certainly wasn't going to warn him. Serve Henry right.

Well, if Peter was spying on Margaret for Henry,

Susan certainly wasn't going to warn her. Serve
Margaret right.

Dungeon Drinks, eh?

Margaret liked that idea much better than her
stinkbomb plot.

'I've changed my mind about the stinkbomb,' said
Margaret. 'I'm going to swap his drinks for Dungeon
Drink stinkers instead.'

'Good idea,' said Lazy Linda. 'Less work.'

Stinkbomb, eh?

Henry liked that much better than his dungeon
drink plot. Why hadn't he thought of that himself?

'I've changed my mind about the Dungeon
Drinks,' said Henry. 'I'm going to stinkbomb her
instead.'

'Yeah,' said Rude Ralph. 'When?'

'Now,' said Horrid Henry. 'Come on, let's go to my
room.'

Horrid Henry opened his Stinky Stinkbomb kit. He'd bought it with Grandma. Mum would *never* have let him buy it. But because Grandma had given him the money Mum couldn't do anything about it. Ha ha ha.

Now, which pong would he pick? He looked at the test tubes filled with powder and read the gruesome labels.

Bad breath. Dog poo. Rotten eggs. Smelly socks. Dead fish. Sewer stench.

'I'd go for dead fish,' said Ralph. 'That's the worst.'

Henry considered.

'How about we mix dead fish *and* rotten eggs?'

'Yeah,' said Rude Ralph.

Slowly, carefully, Horrid Henry measured out a teaspoon of Dead Fish powder, and a teaspoon of Rotten Egg powder, into the special pouch.

Slowly, carefully, Rude Ralph poured out 150 millilitres of secret stinkbomb liquid into the bottle and capped it tightly.

All they had to do was to add the powder to the bottle outside the Secret Club and— run!

'Ready?' said Horrid Henry.

'Ready,' said Rude Ralph.

'Whatever you do,' said Horrid Henry, 'don't spill it.'

'So you've come crawling back,' said Moody Margaret. 'I knew you would.'

'No,' said Sour Susan. 'I just happened to be passing.'
She looked around the Secret Club Tent.

'Where's Linda?'

Margaret scowled. 'Gone.'

'Gone for today, or gone for ever?' said Susan.

'For ever,' said Margaret savagely. 'I don't ever want to see that lazy lump again.'

Margaret and Susan looked at each other.

Susan tapped her foot.

Margaret hummed.

'Well?' said Margaret.

'Well what?' said Susan.

'Are you rejoining the Secret Club as Chief Spy or aren't you?'

'I might,' said Susan. 'And I might not.'

'Suit yourself,' said Margaret. 'I'll call Gurinder and ask her to join instead.'

'Okay,' said Susan quickly. 'I'll join.'

Should she mention her visit to Henry? Better not. After all, what Margaret didn't know wouldn't hurt her.

'Now, about my stinkbomb plot,' began Margaret. 'I decided –'

Something shattered on the ground inside the tent. A ghastly, gruesome, grisly stinky stench filled the air.

'AAAAARGGGGG!' screamed Margaret, gagging.

'It's a — STINKBOMB!'

'HELP!' shrieked Sour Susan. 'STINKBOMB! Help! Help!'

Victory! Horrid Henry and Rude Ralph ran back to the Purple Hand Fort and rolled round the floor, laughing and shrieking.

What a triumph! Margaret and Susan screaming! Margaret's mum screaming! Margaret's dad screaming! And the stink! Wow! Horrid Henry had never smelled anything so awful in his life.

This called for a celebration.

Horrid Henry offered Ralph a fistful of sweets and poured out two glasses of Fizzywizz drinks.

'Cheers!' said Henry.

'Cheers!' said Ralph.

They drank.

'AAAAAARRGGGGGG!' choked Rude Ralph.

'Bleeeeeech!' yelped Horrid Henry, gagging and spitting. 'We've been –' cough! '– Dungeon-Drinked!'

And then Horrid Henry heard a horrible sound. Moody Margaret and Sour Susan were outside the Purple Hand Fort. Chanting a victory chant:

'NAH NAH NE NAH NAH!'

EVIL ENEMY

Perfect Peter

KVGVI RH Z HNVOOB GLZW DLIN.

TOP SECRET PHRASE BOOK

Peter is smelly = **Hi!**

Peter is a worm = **Give me all your pocket money.**

Nappy-Face Toad = **I want biscuits.**

Peter is the Duke of Poop = **Goodbye!**

Example:

Peter is smelly. Peter is a worm.
Peter is the Duke of Poop.
means
Hi! Give me all your pocket money. Goodbye!

(So I'm NOT calling Peter names. I'm just talking in code.)

MOODY MARGARET CASTS A SPELL

'Y ou are getting sleepy,' said Moody Margaret. 'You are getting very sleepy . . .'

Slowly she waved her watch in front of Susan.

'So sleepy . . . you are now asleep . . . you are now fast asleep . . .'

'No I'm not,' said Sour Susan.

'When I click my fingers you will start snoring.'

Margaret clicked her fingers.

'But I'm not asleep,' said Susan.

Margaret glared at her.

Peter is smelly

'How am I supposed to hypnotise you if you don't try?' said Margaret.

'I *am* trying, you're just a bad hypnotist,' said Susan sourly. 'Now it's my turn.'

'No it's not, it's still mine,' said Margaret.

'You've had your go,' said Susan.

'No I haven't!'

'But I never get to be the hypnotist!' wailed Susan.

'Cry baby!'

'Meanie!'

'Cheater!'

'Cheater!'

Slap!

Slap!

Susan glared at Margaret. Why was

she friends with such a mean moody bossyboots?

Margaret glared at Susan. Why was she friends with such a stupid sour sulker?

'I hate you, Margaret!' screamed Sour Susan.

'I hate you more!' screamed Moody Margaret.

'Shut up, landlubbers!' shrieked Horrid Henry from his hammock in the garden next door. 'Or the Purple Hand will make you walk the plank!'

'Shut up yourself, Henry,' said Margaret.

'Yeah, Henry,' said Susan.

'You are stupid, you are stupid,' chanted Rude Ralph, who was playing pirates with Henry.

'You're the stupids,' snapped Moody Margaret. 'Now leave us alone, we're busy.'

'Henry, can I play pirates with you?' asked Perfect Peter, wandering out from the house.

'No, you puny prawn!' screamed

Captain Hook. 'Out of my way before I tear you to pieces with my hook!'

'Muuum,' wailed Peter. 'Henry said he was going to tear me to pieces!'

'Stop being horrid, Henry!' shouted Mum.

'And he won't let me play with him,' said Peter.

'Can't you be nice to your brother for once?' said Dad.

NO! thought Horrid Henry. Why should he be nice to that tell-tale brat?

Horrid Henry did not want to play pirates with Peter. Peter was the world's worst pirate. He couldn't swordfight. He couldn't swashbuckle. He couldn't remember pirate curses. All he could do was whine.

'Okay, Peter, you're the prisoner. Wait in the fort,' said Henry.

'But I'm always the prisoner,' said Peter.

Henry glared at him.

'Do you want to play or don't you?'

'Yes Captain,' said Peter. He crawled into the lair of the Purple Hand. Being prisoner was better than nothing, he supposed. He just hoped he wouldn't have to wait too long.

'Let's get out of here quick,' Henry whispered to Rude Ralph. 'I've got a great idea for playing a trick on Margaret and Susan.' He whispered to Ralph. Ralph grinned.

Horrid Henry hoisted himself onto the low brick wall between his garden and Margaret's.

Moody Margaret was still waving her watch at Susan. Unfortunately, Susan had her back turned and her arms folded.

'Go away, Henry,' ordered Margaret.

'Yeah Henry,' said Susan. 'No boys.'

'Are you being hypnotists?' said Henry.

'Margaret's trying to hypnotise me, only she can't 'cause she's a rubbish hypnotist,' said Susan.

'That's your fault,' said Margaret, glaring.

'Of course you can't hypnotise her,' said Henry. 'You're doing it all wrong.'

'And what would you know about that?' asked Margaret.

'Because,' said Horrid Henry, 'I am a master hypnotist.'

Moody Margaret laughed.

'He is too a master hypnotist,' said Ralph. 'He hypnotises me all the time.'

'Oh yeah?' said Margaret.

'Yeah,' said Henry.

'Prove it,' said Margaret.

'Okay,' said Horrid Henry. 'Gimme the watch.'

Margaret handed it over.

He turned to Ralph.

'Look into my eyes,' he ordered.

Ralph looked into Henry's eyes.

'Now watch the watch,' ordered Henry the hypnotist, swinging the watch back and forth. Rude Ralph swayed.

'You will obey my commands,' said Henry.

'I – will – obey,' said Ralph in a robot voice.

'When I whistle, you will jump off the wall,' said Henry. He whistled.

Ralph jumped off the wall.

'See?' said Horrid Henry.

'That doesn't prove he's hypnotised,' said Margaret. 'You have to make him do silly things.'

'Like what?' said Henry.

'Tell him he's got no clothes on.'

'Ralph, you're a nudie,' said Henry.

Ralph immediately started running round the garden shrieking.

'Aaaaaaarrgghh!' yelped Ralph. 'I'm a nudie! I'm a nudie! Give me some clothes, help help! No one look, I'm naked!'

Margaret hesitated. There was no way Henry could

have *really* hypnotised Ralph – was there?

'I still don't believe he's hypnotised,' said Margaret.

'Then watch this,' said Horrid Henry. 'Ralph – when I snap my fingers you will be . . . Margaret.'

Snap!

'My name is Margaret,' said Ralph. 'I'm a mean bossyboots. I'm the biggest bossiest boot. I'm a frogface.'

Margaret blushed red.

Susan giggled.

'It's not funny,' snapped Margaret. *No one* made fun of her and lived to tell the tale.

'See?' said Henry. 'He obeys my every command.'

'Wow,' said Susan. 'You really are a hypnotist. Can you teach me?'

'Maybe,' said Horrid Henry. 'How much will you pay me?'

'He's just a big faker,' said Margaret. She stuck her nose in the air. 'If you're such a great hypnotist, then hypnotise *me*.'

Oops. Now he was trapped. Margaret was trying to spoil his trick. Well, no way would he let her.

Horrid Henry remembered who he was. The boy who got Miss Battle-Axe sent to the head. The boy who terrified the bogey babysitter. The boy who tricked the Tooth Fairy. He could hypnotise Margaret any day.

'Sure,' he said, waving the watch in front of Margaret.

'You are getting sleepy,' droned Henry. 'You are getting very sleepy. When I snap my fingers you will obey my every command.'

Henry snapped his fingers. Margaret glared at him.

'Well?' said Moody Margaret.

'Don't you know *anything*?' said Horrid Henry. He thought fast. 'That was just the beginning bit. I will complete part two once I have freed Ralph from my power. Ralph, repeat after me, 'I am sellotape'.'

'I am sellotape,' said Rude Ralph. Then he belched.

'I am burping sellotape,' said Rude Ralph. He caught Henry's eye. They burst out laughing.

'Ha ha, Susan, fooled you!' shrieked Henry.

'Did not,' shrieked Susan.

'Did too. Nah nah ne nah nah!' Henry and Ralph ran round Margaret, whooping and cheering.

'Come on Margaret,' said Susan. 'Let's go and do some *real* hypnosis.'

Margaret didn't move.

'Come on, Margaret,' said Susan.

'I am sellotape,' said Margaret.

'No you're not,' said Susan.

'Yes I am,' said Margaret.

Henry and Ralph stopped whooping.

'There's something wrong with Margaret,' said Susan. 'She's acting all funny. Margaret, are you okay? Margaret? Margaret?'

Moody Margaret stood very still. Her eyes looked blank.

Horrid Henry snapped his fingers.

'Raise your right arm,' he ordered.

Margaret raised her right arm.

Huh? thought Horrid Henry.

'Pinch Susan.'

Margaret pinched Susan.

'Owww!' yelped Susan.

'Repeat after me, 'I am a stupid girl'.'

'I am a stupid girl,' said Margaret.

'No you're not,' said Susan.

'Yes I am,' said Margaret.

'She's hypnotised,' said Horrid Henry. He'd actually hypnotised Moody Margaret. This was amazing. This was fantastic. He really truly was a master hypnotist!

'Will you obey me, slave?'

'I will obey,' said Margaret.

'When I click my fingers, you will be a . . . chicken.'

Click!

'Squawk! Squawk! Squawk!' cackled Margaret, flapping her arms wildly.

'What have you done to her?' wailed Sour Susan.

'Wow,' said Rude Ralph. 'You've hypnotised her.'

Horrid Henry could not believe his luck. If he could hypnotise Margaret, he could hypnotise anyone. Everyone would have to obey his commands. He would be master of the world! The universe! Everything!

Henry could see it now.

'Henry, ten out of ten,' Miss Battle-Axe would say. 'Henry is so clever he doesn't ever need to do homework again.'

Oh boy, would he fix Miss Battle-Axe.

He'd make her do the hula in a grass skirt when she wasn't running round the playground mooing like a cow.

He'd make the head, Mrs Oddbod, just have chocolate and cake for school dinners. And no P.E. – ever. In fact, he'd make Mrs Oddbod close down the school.

And as for Mum and Dad . . .

'Henry, have as many sweets as you like,' Dad would say.

'No bedtime for you,' Mum would say.

'Henry, watch as much TV as you want,' Dad would say.

'Henry, here's your pocket money – £1000 a week. Tell us if you need more,' Mum would smile.

'Peter, go to your room and stay there for a year!' Mum and Dad would scream.

Henry would hypnotise them all later. But first, what should he make Margaret do?

Ah yes. Her house was filled with sweets and biscuits and fizzy drinks – all the things Henry's horrible parents never let him have.

'Bring us all your sweets, all your biscuits and a Fizzywizz drink.'

'Yes, master,' said Moody Margaret.

Henry stretched out in the hammock. So did Rude Ralph. This was the life!

Sour Susan didn't know what to do. On the one hand, Margaret was mean and horrible, and she hated her. It was fun watching her obey orders for once. On the other hand, Susan would much rather Margaret was *her* slave than Henry's.

'Unhypnotise her, Henry,' said Sour Susan.

'Soon,' said Horrid Henry.

'Let's hypnotise Peter next,' said Ralph.

'Yeah,' said Henry. No more telling tales. No more goody goody vegetable-eating I'm Mr Perfect. Oh boy would he hypnotise Peter!

Moody Margaret came slowly out of her house. She was carrying a large pitcher and a huge bowl of chocolate mousse.

'Here is your Fizzywizz drink, master,' said

Margaret. Then she poured it on top of him.

'Wha? Wha?' spluttered Henry, gasping and choking.

'And your dinner, frogface,' she added, tipping the mousse all over Ralph.

'Ugggh!' wailed Ralph.

'NAH NAH NE NAH NAH,' shrieked Margaret. 'Fooled you! Fooled you!'

Perfect Peter crept out of the Purple Hand Fort. What was all that yelling? It must be a pirate mutiny!

'Hang on pirates, here I come!' shrieked Peter, charging at the thrashing hammock as fast as he could.

CRASH!

A sopping wet pirate captain and a mousse-covered

first mate lay on the ground. They stared up at their prisoner.

'Hi Henry,' said Peter. 'I mean, hi Captain.' He took a step backwards. 'I mean, Lord High Excellent Majesty.' He took another step back.

'Ugh, we were playing pirate mutiny – weren't we?'

'DIE, WORM!' yelled Horrid Henry, leaping up.

'MUUUUUUM!' shrieked Peter.

Ha ha Henry! Gotcha!
Our dungeon drink trick
was much better than your
stupid stinkbomb.
Nah Nah Ne Nah Nah
The Secret Club rules!

HOW TO BE A MASTER HYPNOTIST

in 3 easy steps

1 Wave a watch in front of the person you want to hypnotise.

2 Tell them, 'You are getting sleepy. You are getting very sleepy. You are now asleep.'

3 Snap your fingers and order them to be your slave !!!

Z GZIZMGFOZ ZGVIVYVXXZ.SZ SZ SZ.

HFHZM SZH KLMTB KZMGH.
Susan has pongy pants.

NZITZIVG RH Z KLGZGL.
Margaret is a potato.

YROO SZH Z YRT SFTV TRMLI NLFH YLGGLN.
Bill has a big huge ginormous bottom.

Z GZIZMGFOZ ZGV IVYVXXZ. SZ SZ SZ.
A tarantula ate Rebecca. HA HA HA.

NRHH YZGGOV-ZCV VZGH MRGH.
Miss Battle-Axe eats nits.

HNVOOB GLZW YILGSVIH PVVK LFG.
Smelly toad brothers keep out.

HGVEV RH HGFXP-FK, BFXPB ZMW SLIIRYOV.
Steve is stuck-up, yucky and horrible.

KVGVI RH Z HNVOOB GLZW DLIN.
Peter is a smelly toad worm.

R DZMG Z PROOVI XZGZKFOG ZMW YLLN-YLLN YZHSVI.
I want a killer catapult and boom-boom basher.

HORRID HENRY
AND THE
BOGEY BABYSITTER

'No way!' shrieked Tetchy Tess, slamming down the phone.

'No way!' shrieked Crabby Chris, slamming down the phone.

'No way!' shrieked Angry Anna. 'What do you think I am, crazy?'

Even Mellow Martin said he was busy.

Mum hung up the phone and groaned.

It wasn't easy finding someone to babysit more than once for Horrid Henry. When Tetchy Tess came, Henry flooded the bathroom. When Crabby Chris came he hid her homework and 'accidentally' poured red grape juice down the front of her new white jeans. And when Angry Anna came Henry – no, it's too dreadful. Suffice it to say that Anna ran screaming from the house and Henry's parents had to come home early.

Horrid Henry hated babysitters. He wasn't a baby. He didn't want to be sat on. Why should he be nice to some ugly, stuck-up, bossy teenager who'd hog the TV and pig out on Henry's biscuits? Parents should just stay at home where they belonged, thought Horrid Henry.

And now it looked like they would have to. Ha! His parents were mean and horrible, but he'd had a lot of

practice managing them. Babysitters were unpredictable. Babysitters were hard work. And by the time you'd broken them in and shown them who was boss, for some reason they didn't want to come any more. The only good babysitters let you stay up all night and eat sweets until you were sick. Sadly, Horrid Henry never got one of those.

'We have to find a babysitter,' wailed Mum. 'The party is tomorrow night. I've tried everyone. Who else is there?'

'There's got to be someone,' said Dad. 'Think!'

Mum thought.

Dad thought.

'What about Rebecca?' said Dad.

Horrid Henry's heart missed a beat. He stopped drawing moustaches on Perfect Peter's school pictures. Maybe he'd heard wrong. Oh please, not

Rebecca! Not – Rabid Rebecca!

'Who did you say?' asked Henry. His voice quavered.

'You heard me,' said Dad. 'Rebecca.'

'NO!' screamed Henry. 'She's horrible!'

'She's not horrible,' said Dad. 'She's just – strict.'

'There's no one else,' said Mum grimly. 'I'll phone Rebecca.'

'She's a monster!' wailed Henry. 'She made Ralph go to bed at six o'clock!'

'I like going to bed at six o'clock,' said Perfect Peter. 'After all, growing children need their rest.'

Horrid Henry growled and attacked. He was the Creature from the Black Lagoon, dragging the foolish mortal down to a watery grave.

'AAAEEEEE!' squealed Peter. 'Henry pulled my hair.'

'Stop being horrid, Henry!' said Dad. 'Mum's on the phone.'

Henry prayed. Maybe she'd be busy. Maybe she'd say no. Maybe she'd be dead. He'd heard all about Rebecca. She'd made Tough Toby get in his pyjamas at five o'clock *and* do all his homework. She'd unplugged Dizzy Dave's computer. She'd made Moody Margaret wash the floor. No doubt about it, Rabid Rebecca was the toughest teen in town.

Henry lay on the rug and howled. Mum shouted into the phone.

'You can! That's great, Rebecca. No, that's just the TV – sorry for the noise. See you tomorrow.'

'NOOOOOOOOO!' wailed Henry.

Ding dong.

'I'll get it!' said Perfect Peter. He skipped to the door.

Henry flung himself on the carpet.

'I DON'T WANT TO HAVE A BABYSITTER!' he wailed.

The door opened. In walked the biggest, meanest, ugliest, nastiest-looking girl Henry had ever seen. Her arms were enormous. Her head was enormous. Her teeth were enormous. She looked like she ate elephants for breakfasts, crocodiles for lunch, and snacked on toddlers for tea.

'What have you got to eat?' snarled Rabid Rebecca.

Dad took a step back. 'Help yourself to anything in the fridge,' said Dad.

'Don't worry, I will,' said Rebecca.

'GO HOME, YOU WITCH!' howled Henry.

'Bedtime is nine o'clock,' shouted Dad, trying to be heard above Henry's screams. He edged his way carefully past Rebecca, jumped over Henry, then dashed out the front door.

'I DON'T WANT TO HAVE A BABYSITTER!' shrieked Henry.

'Be good, Henry,' said Mum weakly. She stepped

over Henry, then escaped from the house.

The door closed.

Horrid Henry was alone in the house with Rabid Rebecca.

He glared at Rebecca.

Rebecca glared at him.

'I've heard all about you, you little creep,' growled Rebecca. 'No one bothers me when I'm babysitting.'

Horrid Henry stopped screaming.

'Oh yeah,' said Horrid Henry. 'We'll see about that.'

Rabid Rebecca bared her fangs. Henry recoiled. Perhaps I'd better keep out of her way, he thought, then slipped into the sitting room and turned on the telly.

Ahh, Mutant Max. Hurray! How bad could life be when a brilliant programme like Mutant Max was on? He'd annoy Rebecca as soon as it was over.

Rebecca stomped into the room and snatched the clicker.

ZAP!

DA DOO, DA DOO DA, DA DOO DA DOO DA,

tangoed some horrible spangly dancers.

'Hey,' said Henry. 'I'm watching Mutant Max.'

'Tough,' said Rebecca. '*I'm* watching ballroom dancing.'

Snatch!

Horrid Henry grabbed the clicker.

ZAP!

'And it's mutants, mutants, mut – '

Snatch!

Zap!

DA DOO, DA DOO DA, DA DOO DA DOODA. DOO, DA DOO DA, DA DOO DA DOO DA.

Horrid Henry tangoed round the room, gliding and sliding.

'Stop it,' muttered Rebecca.

Henry shimmied back and forth in front of the telly, blocking her view and singing along as loudly as he could.

'DA DOO, DA DOO DA,' warbled Henry.

'I'm warning you,' hissed Rebecca.

Perfect Peter walked in. He had already put on his blue bunny pyjamas,

brushed his teeth and combed his hair. He held a game of Chinese Checkers in his hand.

'Rebecca, will you play a game with me before I go to bed?' asked Peter.

'NO!' roared Rebecca. 'I'm trying to watch TV. Shut up and go away.'

Perfect Peter leapt back.

'But I thought – since I was all ready for bed – he stammered.

'I've got better things to do than to play with you,' snarled Rebecca. 'Now go to bed this minute, both of you.'

'But it's not my bedtime for hours,' protested Henry. 'I want to watch Mutant Max.'

'Nor mine,' said Perfect Peter timidly. 'There's this nature programme – '

'GO!' howled Rebecca.

'NO!' howled Henry.

'RAAAAA!' roared Rabid Rebecca.

Horrid Henry did not know how it happened. It was as if fiery dragon's breath had blasted him upstairs. Somehow, he was in his pyjamas, in bed, and it was only seven o'clock.

Nappy-Face Toad

Rabid Rebecca switched off the light. 'Don't even think of moving from that bed,' she hissed. 'If I see you, or hear you, or even smell you, you'll be sorry you were born. I'll stay downstairs, you stay upstairs, and that way no one will get hurt.' Then she marched out of the room and slammed the door.

Horrid Henry was so shocked he could not move. He, Horrid Henry, the bulldozer of babysitters, the terror of teachers, the bully of brothers, was in bed, lights out, at seven o'clock.

Seven o'clock! Two whole hours before his bedtime! This was an outrage! He could hear Moody Margaret shrieking next door. He could hear Toddler Tom zooming about on his tricycle. No one went to bed at seven o'clock. Not even toddlers!

Worst of all, he was thirsty. So what if

177

she told me to stay in bed, thought Horrid Henry. I'm thirsty. I'm going to go downstairs and get myself a glass of water. It's my house and I'll do what I want.

Horrid Henry did not move.

I'm dying of thirst here, thought Henry. Mum and Dad will come home and I'll be a dried out old stick insect, and boy will she be in trouble.

Horrid Henry still did not move.

Go on, feet, urged Henry, let's just step on down and get a little ol' glass of water. So what if that bogey babysitter said he had to stay in bed. What could she do to him?

She could chop off my
head and bounce it down
the stairs, thought Henry.

Eeek.

Well, let her try.

Horrid Henry
remembered who he
was. The boy who'd sent
teachers shrieking from the
classroom. The boy who'd destroyed the Demon
Dinner Lady. The boy who had run away from home
and almost reached the Congo.

I will get up and get a drink of water, he thought.

Sneak.

Sneak.

Sneak.

Horrid Henry crept to the
bedroom door.

Slowly he opened it a crack.

Creak.

Then slowly, slowly, he opened
the door a bit more and slipped out.

ARGHHHHHH!

There was Rabid Rebecca sitting
at the top of the stairs.

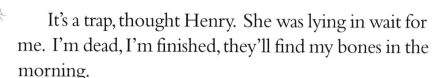

It's a trap, thought Henry. She was lying in wait for me. I'm dead, I'm finished, they'll find my bones in the morning.

Horrid Henry dashed back inside his room and awaited his doom.

Silence.

What was going on? Why hadn't Rebecca torn him apart limb from limb?

Horrid Henry opened his door a fraction and peeped out.

Rabid Rebecca was still sitting huddled at the top of the stairs. She did not move. Her eyes were fixed straight ahead.

'Spi–spi–spider,' she whispered. She pointed at a big, hairy spider in front of her with a trembling hand.

'It's huge,' said Henry. 'Really hairy and horrible and wriggly and –'

'STOP!' squealed Rebecca. 'Help me, Henry,' she begged.

Horrid Henry was not the fearless leader of a pirate

gang for nothing.

'If I risk my life and get rid of the spider, can I watch Mutant Max?' said Henry.

'Yes,' said Rebecca.

'And stay up till my parents come home?'

'Yes,' said Rebecca.

'And eat all the ice cream in the fridge?'

'YES!' shrieked Rebecca. 'Just get rid of that — that —'

'Deal,' said Horrid Henry.

He dashed to his room and grabbed a jar.

Rabid Rebecca hid her eyes as Horrid Henry scooped up the spider. What a beauty!

'It's gone,' said Henry.

Rebecca opened her beady red eyes.

'Right, back to bed, you little brat!'

'What?' said Henry.

'Bed. Now!' screeched Rebecca.

'But we agreed . . .' said Henry.

'Tough,' said Rebecca. 'That was then.'

'Traitor,' said Henry.

He whipped out the spider jar from behind his back and unscrewed the lid.

'On guard!' he said.

'AAEEEE!' whimpered Rebecca.

Horrid Henry advanced menacingly towards her.

'NOOOOOOO!' wailed Rebecca, stepping back.

'Now get in that room and stay there,' ordered Henry. 'Or else.'

Rabid Rebecca skedaddled into the bathroom and locked the door.

'If I see you or hear you or even smell you you'll be sorry you were born,' said Henry.

'I already am,' said Rabid Rebecca.

Horrid Henry spent a lovely evening in front of the telly. He watched scary movies. He ate ice cream and sweets and biscuits and crisps until he could stuff no more in.

Vroom vroom.

Oops. Parents home.

Horrid Henry dashed upstairs and leapt into bed just as the front door opened.

Mum and Dad looked around the sitting room, littered with sweet wrappers, biscuit crumbs and ice cream cartons.

'You did tell her to help herself,' said Mum.

'Still,' said Dad. 'What a pig.'

'Never mind,' said Mum brightly, 'at least she managed to get Henry to bed. That's a first.'

Rabid Rebecca staggered into the room.

'Did you get enough to eat?' said Dad.

'No,' said Rabid Rebecca.

'Oh,' said Dad.

'Was everything all right?' asked Mum.

Rebecca looked at her.

'Can I go now?' said Rebecca.

'Any chance you could babysit on Saturday?' asked Dad hopefully.

'What do you think I am, crazy?' shrieked Rebecca. SLAM!

184

Upstairs, Horrid Henry groaned.

Rats. It was so unfair. Just when he had a babysitter beautifully trained, for some reason they wouldn't come back.

EVIL ENEMY

Rabid Rebecca

EVIL ENEMIES FACT FILE

Worst enemies

Peter
Nickname: Perfect
Worst features:
too many to count
Best feature: none
Most evil crime:
being born

Margaret
Nickname: Moody
Worst features:
grouchy, bossy
Best feature: owns a
pirate hook, sabre and
cutlass
Most evil crime:
living next door

Susan

Nickname: Sour
Worst feature:
whining, moaning
copycat
Best feature: slaps
Margaret
Most evil crime:
joining Margaret's
secret club

Steve

Nickname: Stuck-up
Worst feature:
always bragging
about how rich he is
Best feature: lives
far away
Most evil crime:
trying to trick me
into thinking his
house was haunted

Bill

Nickname: Bossy
Worst feature:
mean, double-
crossing creep
Best feature:
doesn't go to my
school

Most evil crime: getting me into trouble
at Dad's office

Rebecca

Nickname: Rabid
Worst features:
toughest teen in town.
Makes children go to
bed early and hogs
the TV.
Best feature: scared
of spiders
Most evil crime: making me go to bed at 7
pm!!

Lily

Nickname: Lisping
Worst feature: follows me around
Best feature: smaller than me
Most evil crime: asking me to marry her

Worst babysitters

Tetchy Tess
Crabby Chris
Angry Anna
Rabid Rebecca

Other things I hate

Homework
Boring holidays
Walks
Fresh air
Healthy food
Bedtime

Greatest victories

Tricking Bossy Bill into photocopying his bottom
Switching Christmas presents with Stuck-up Steve
Stinkbombing Moody Margaret's Secret Club
Enlisting Sour Susan as a double agent
Defeating Rabid Rebecca
Escaping Lisping Lily
Being older, bigger and cleverer than Perfect Peter

Peter is the Duke of Poop

HORRID HENRY

by Francesca Simon

Illustrated by Tony Ross

HORRID HENRY

HORRID HENRY AND THE SECRET CLUB

HORRID HENRY TRICKS THE TOOTH FAIRY

HORRID HENRY'S NITS

HORRID HENRY GETS RICH QUICK

HORRID HENRY'S REVENGE

HORRID HENRY'S HAUNTED HOUSE

HORRID HENRY AND THE MUMMY'S CURSE

HORRID HENRY AND THE BOGEY BABYSITTER

HORRID HENRY'S STINKBOMB

HORRID HENRY'S UNDERPANTS

HORRID HENRY MEETS THE QUEEN

HORRID HENRY'S JOKE BOOK

HORRID HENRY AND THE THE MEGA-MEAN TIME MACHINE

HORRID HENRY AND THE FOOTBALL FIEND

HORRID HENRY'S BIG BAD BOOK

a big book of stories about Horrid Henry at school,
with colour pictures and new information –
just like this one!

HORRID HENRY'S WICKED WAYS

a second big book of stories about Henry at home.

Look out for
HORRID HENRY'S CHRISTMAS CRACKER

*All the storybooks are available on audio cassette
and CD, read by Miranda Richardson*